SUPER EXPERT
MATHS QUIZ

SUPER EXPERT
MATHS QUIZ

DILIP M. SALWI

RUPA

To my friend and well-wisher, Dr N.R. Mankad,
for his humane qualities.

Published by
Rupa Publications India Pvt. Ltd 2004
7/16, Ansari Road, Daryaganj
New Delhi 110002

Sales centres:

Allahabad Bengaluru Chennai
Hyderabad Jaipur Kathmandu
Kolkata Mumbai

ISBN: 978-81-716-7010-9

Eighth impression 2019

10 9 8

Hello! Mathematics Quiz Buffs!

Could there be 'Mathematics quiz buffs'? One may wonder when mathematics does not figure in any television programme, radio or newspaper column. But I am sure they are present, though they must be in minority. Why am I so confident about their invisible presence? You may ask. There is one simple reason. My '1000 Maths Quiz' first published in 1989 has ran into more than than 13 editions! Quite a phenomenal response to a subject considered at large to be cut and dry. Obviously, it shows there is a select gentry who is seriously interested in mathematics.

Be that as it may, I reiterate here that in the process of revising and updating '1000 Maths Quiz' I have split it into two handy books with some new questions (not much has changed in mathematics over the last decade) but at the same time retaining the wholistic spirit in both. They have also been renamed 'Super Expert Maths Quiz' and 'Super Genius Maths Quiz' so that they become part of the 'Super quiz series' I have written for kids and children. I have increased questions concerning computers and added new ones on the emerging field of computer software and internet as both are offshoots of mathematics. Of course, all questions posed have direct relevance to mathematics.

I am sure these two books would further stimulate interest in mathematics. After going through them nobody would consider the subject not enjoyable or irrelevant to society or daily life. If some of my mathematics buffs go on to pursue mathematics as a career, my purpose in writing these books would be more than fulfilled.

July 31, 2003   Dilip M. Salwi

CONTENTS

I

FIRST THINGS FIRST

First Mathematicians

1. Who is considered to be the first modern mathematician?
   (a) Rene Descartes   (b) Pierre de Fermat
   (c) Isaac Barrow   (d) William Oughtred

2. Who built the first electronic calculating machine?
   (a) John W. Mauchly   (b) J. Presper Eckert
   (c) John V. Atanasoff   (d) Konrad Zuse

3. Who made the first attempt to explain the behaviour of gases mathematically with respect to changing pressure and temperature?
   (a) Anders Celsius   (b) Robert Boyle
   (c) Jacques Charles   (d) Daniel Bernoulli

4. Who was the first to apply statistics to investigations in biology?
   (a) Gregor Mendel
   (b) Francis Galton
   (c) Charles Darwin
   (d) Thomas Malthus

5. Who was the first to apply mathematics to understand economic problems?
   (a) John Maynard Keynes
   (b) William Stanley Jevons
   (c) Alfred Marshall
   (d) Alfredo Pareto

6. Who invented the first mechanical calculator?
   (a) Wilhelm Schickard
   (b) Blaise Pascal
   (c) John Napier
   (d) William Oughtred

7. Who is the first person to give stage performances for his/her mental calculating abilities?
   (a) Shakuntala Devi
   (b) Zerah Colburn
   (c) George Parker Bidder
   (d) Alexender Craig Aitken

8. Who was the first person to visualise a comforting picture of complex numbers in a two-dimensional plane?
   (a) Jean Robert Argand
   (b) Carl F. Gauss
   (c) Caspar Wessel
   (d) Charles Steinmetz

9. Who was the first European to advocate the use of the decimal number system in mathematical calculations?
   (a) Benjamin Franklin　　(b) Simon Steven
   (c) Robert Recorde　　(d) Micheal Stifel

10. Who was the first modern mathematician to have contributed to both pure and applied mathematics?
    (a) Paul Erdos　　(b) Carl F. Gauss
    (c) Leonard Euler
    (d) Pierre Simon Laplace

11. Who wrote the first Latin treatise *Ars magna* solely devoted to algebra?
    (a) Nicolo Tartaglia　　(b) Girolamo Cardano
    (c) Francois Viete　　(d) Christopher Clavius

12. Who was the first mathematician to apply mathematics to the science of artillery?
    (a) Nicolo Tartaglia　　(b) Galileo Galilei
    (c) Diophantus　　(d) Archimedes

13. Who was the first mathematician to calculate the value of π (pi) ?
    (a) Aristotle　　(b) Euclid
    (c) Aryabhata　　(d) Archimedes

14. Who was the first mathematician to give the approximate value of π (pi) which is commonly accepted today?
    - (a) Al-Kashi
    - (b) Aryabhata
    - (c) Tsu Ch'ung-chih
    - (d) Claudius Ptolemy

15. Who built the first Analogue mechanical calculator?
    - (a) Lord Kelvin
    - (b) Edvard Scheutz
    - (c) Ramon Verea
    - (d) Dorr Felt

16. Who was the first mathematician to take seriously the editing and publishing of writings of other mathematicians?
    - (a) Jean Bernoulli
    - (b) G. W. Leibniz
    - (c) J. J. Sylvester
    - (d) Gabriel Cramer

17. Who first introduced formal language of symbols in mathematics with the aim of making proofs more rigorous?
    - (a) A. N. Whitehead
    - (b) Gottlob Frege
    - (c) George Boole
    - (d) Christian Kramp

First Things

18. Which is the first printed book on mathematics?
    - (a) *Leelavati*
    - (b) *On the Sphere and Cylinder*
    - (c) *Arithmetica*
    - (d) *Treviso Arithmetic*

19. Which is the first irrational number to be discovered?
    - (a) $\sqrt{3}$
    - (b) $\sqrt{2}$
    - (c) $\sqrt{8}$
    - (d) $\sqrt{15}$

20. Whose book contained the decimal point in the present form for the first time?
    - (a) John Napier
    - (b) Simon Steven
    - (c) Al-Kashi
    - (d) Auguste Comte

21. Which computer was used for the first time to calculate the exact value of π ?
    - (a) ENIAC
    - (b) Bush's Differential Analyser
    - (c) MANIAC
    - (d) CRAY-I

22. Which is the first number starting from 1 both 'interesting' and 'uninteresting'?
    - (a) 8
    - (b) 81
    - (c) 39
    - (d) 154

23. Where did complex numbers first find scientific application in?
    - (a) Electricity
    - (b) Magnetism
    - (c) Electrostatics
    - (d) Optics

24. Which is the first 'abundant' number?
    - (a) 12
    - (b) 16
    - (c) 30
    - (d) 22

25. Rabbits appeared for the first and the last time in this famous mathematical item. What is it?
    - (a) Mersenne numbers
    - (b) Napier's bones
    - (c) Fibonacci sequence
    - (d) Mandelbrot fractuals

26. It is the first book which contained algebra as we know it today and which led to the development of symbolic algebra. Which is it?
    - (a) *Isogoge in artem analyticam*
    - (b) *Liber quadratorum*
    - (c) *Spherics*
    - (d) *Mathematical Collection*

27. Which is the first composite number?
    - (a) 4
    - (b) 3
    - (c) 6
    - (d) 120

28. What was the subject of the first computer programme created by Ada Lovelace ?
    (a) Kaprekar's numbers
    (b) Bernoulli numbers
    (c) Pythagoras numbers
    (d) All

II

CREATIVITY AND PERSONALITIES

Mathematical Creativity

29. Who gave the four mathematical paradoxes now famous as Dichotomy, Achilles, Arrow, and Stadium?
    (a) Zeno
    (b) Archimedes
    (c) C. G. Darwin
    (d) C. G. J. Jacobi

30. A mathematician was found good for nothing in various spheres of life. Once on a journey he came across a mathematical problem which he easily solved. It triggered off the mathematician in him. Who was he?
    (a) Joseph Fourier
    (b) Willard V. O. Quine
    (c) John von Neumann
    (d) Simeon Poisson

31. Who is responsible for introducing the idea of 'Proof' in mathematics?
    (a) Democritus   (b) Leucippus
    (c) Euclid   (d) Thales

32. Which mathematician dreamed of reducing ethics, morality and law to mathematical calculations so that even a judge could perform some calculations to arrive at a just decision?
    (a) G. W. Leibniz   (b) Pierre de Fermat
    (c) Imre Lakatos   (d) Nobody

33. Who is practically the last mathematician to make original contributions to both pure and applied mathematics?
    (a) Henri Poincare
    (b) Rene Descartes
    (c) William R. Hamilton
    (d) Isaac Newton

34. Whose book *The Laws of Thoughts* became the basis of computer science?
    (a) George Boole
    (b) Niels Henrik Abel
    (c) David Hilbert
    (d) Kurt Godel

35. Which mathematician was put behind bars and during his stay in prison made an important mathematical discovery?
    (a) Lazare Carnot   (b) Gaspard Monge
    (c) Joseph Louis Language
    (d) Jean Victor Poncelet

36. Who wrote essays like 'Mathematics of war and foreign politics', 'Statistics of deadly quarrels', etc., which gave mathematical interpretations of war?
    (a) Oliver Lodge   (b) Bertrand Russell
    (c) C. E. M. Joad
    (d) Lewis Fry Richardson

37. After fifteen years of fruitless thinking, when a mathematical discovery occurred to him while he was walking on a bridge, he took out a penknife and scratched the discovery on the stone of the bridge. Who was he?
    (a) Arthur Cayley   (b) William R. Hamilton
    (c) George Peacock   (d) Evariste Galois

38. Who used the word 'group' in the mathematical sense for the first time?
    (a) Georg Cantor   (b) Evariste Galois
    (c) Augustin Cauchy   (d) George Boole

39. Which mathematician was killed while he was solving a mathematical problem on sand?
   (a) Euclid　　　　　　　(b) Archimedes
   (c) Conon　　　　　　　(d) Apollonius

40. Which mathematician wrote *The Laws of Verse*?
   (a) J. J. Sylvester　　　　(b) Leopold Kronecker
   (c) Augustin Cauchy　　　(d) William R. Hamilton

41. Who dreamt that mathematics was the 'Open Sesame'?
   (a) Plato　　　　　　　(b) Christian Huygens
   (c) Rene Descartes　　　(d) Leonardo da Vinci

42. This mathematician was so put off by the cold reception given to his work that he took to studying Sanskrit language and literature. Who was he?
   (a) Augustus De Morgan
   (b) Hermann Gunther Grassmann
   (c) Gaspard Monge　　　(d) Jacob Steiner

Personalities

43. Who is often referred to as 'The Copernicus of Geometry'?
   (a) Niels Henrik Abel
   (b) James Joseph Sylvester
   (c) Albert Elinstein
   (d) Nikolai I. Lobatchewsky

44. Which mathematician spent more than a decade of his last days as a blind man ?
    (a) George Boole   (b) Leonard Euler
    (c) Zeno   (d) Richard Dedekind

45. Who is not considered a mathematician but a maker of mathematicians?
    (a) Leonard Euler   (b) Socrates
    (c) Plato   (d) Pythagoras

46. Which eminent mathematician was the son of a gardener and bricklayer?
    (a) Leopold Kronecker
    (b) Johannes Bernoulli
    (c) Carl F. Gauss
    (d) Evariste Galois

47. Whose patent motto in life was 'Whenever you can, count'?
    (a) Karl Pearson   (b) J. B. S. Haldane
    (c) R.A. Fisher   (d) Francis Galois

48. Who is called 'the mathematicians' mathematician'?
    (a) Arthur Cayley
    (b) Neils Henrik Abel
    (c) Lorenzo Mascheroni
    (d) Rene Descartes

49. Which eminent mathematician was always suffering from ill-health?
    (a) Isaac Newton   (b) Leonhard Euler
    (c) Gaspard Monge   (d) Georg F. Riemann

50. Who among the following belonged to a family of mathematicians?
    (a) William R. Hamilton (b) Daniel Bernoulli
    (c) Euclid   (d) Albert Einstein

51. Which mathematician was also a lawyer?
    (a) Blaise Pascal   (b) Pierre de Fermat
    (c) Gottlob Frege   (d) Jacob Bernoulli

52. Whose patent motto was 'Few, but ripe'?
    (a) Karl Weierstrass   (b) Felix Klein
    (c) Georg B. Riemann   (d) Carl F. Gauss

53. Though he made original contributions to mathematics he became a successful businessman too. Who was he?
    (a) Richard Dedekind   (b) Isaac Newton
    (c) Leopold Kronecker   (d) Georg F. Riemann

54. Who is called the 'Prince of mathematicians'?
    (a) Joseph Fourier   (b) William Thomson
    (c) Carl F. Gauss
    (d) Pierre-Simon Laplace

55. Once when a beginner doubted the theory of differential coefficients, this great mathematician of the 18ᵗʰ century said, 'Just go on, and faith will come to you'. Who was he?
    (a) Daniel Bernoulli
    (b) Jacob Bernoulli
    (c) John Couch Adams
    (d) Jean Le Rond D'Alembert

56. Which mathematician once said that he had never done anything useful in his life – even his mathematical discoveries were not of any use to the world?
    (a) J.E. Littlewood   (b) S. Ramanujan
    (c) G. H. Hardy   (d) Simeon Poisson

57. One of the computer-builders and mathematicians was also a long-distance runner. Who was he?
    (a) Simon Gluck   (b) Alan Turing
    (c) F.C. Williams   (d) John von Neumann

III

SOLIDS, CURVES AND TRIANGLES

Solids

58. What is a regular icosahedron made up of?
    (a) 24 Squares
    (b) 15 Equilateral triangles
    (c) 16 Squares
    (d) 20 Equilateral triangles

59. What is this solid called?
    (a) Polyhedron
    (c) Cube

    (b) Octahedron
    (d) Tetrahedron

60. What are these five solids known as ?
    (a) The Euclidean solids
    (b) The Fermatian solids
    (c) The Mahavira solids
    (d) The Platonic solids

61. What is this solid called?

    (a) Dodecahedron   (b) Octahedron
    (c) Tetrahedron   (d) Pyramid

62. Rhombohedron is a six-sided prism. What are its faces?
    (a) Triangles   (b) Squares
    (c) Parallelograms   (d) Trapeziums

63. What is this figure known as?

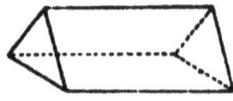

    (a) Tetrahedron   (b) Prism
    (c) Cuboid   (d) Cube

64. What is a regular Octahedron made of?
    (a) Eight squares
    (b) Eight equilateral triangles
    (c) Sixteen squares   (d) Ten polygons

65. Frustum is any part of a cone or pyramid contained between these. What are they?:
    (a) Two parallel planes
    (b) Two non-parallel planes
    (c) Two parallel lines   (d) Three concurrent lines

66. Whose surface area is 2 (ab + bc + ac) (where a, b and c are the lengths of its edges)?
    (a) Pyramid
    (b) Tetrahedron
    (c) Rectangular parallelopiped
    (d) Triangular prism

67. What is this solid called?

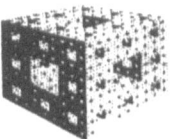

    (a) Hilbert sponge
    (b) Sierpinski sponge
    (c) No name
    (d) Menger sponge

68. What is a regular dodecahedron made up of?
    (a) 12 regular pentagons
    (b) 16 regular pentagons
    (c) 6 regular pentagons
    (d) 16 equilateral triangles

Curves

69. What is this figure known as?

    (a) Witch of Agnesi
    (b) French curve
    (c) Lemniscate
    (d) Crunode

70. Who conceived the following curve ?

(a) J. J. Sylvester   (b) Blaise Pascal
(c) Evariste Galois   (d) Pierre de Fermat

71. When a cup of coffee is kept in the sun, one of the following curves is seen in it. Which one?
(a) Caustic   (b) Spiral
(c) Cosine   (d) Helical

72. The following curve was first made by Blaise Pascal. What is it called ?

(a) Limacon   (b) Pearl
(c) Hippopede   (d) Hyperbola

73. What is the name of this curve?

(a) Epicycloid   (b) Cycloid
(c) Hypocycloid   (d) Trochoid

74. What is a curve in 3-dimensional space known as?
(a) Space curve   (b) Star curve
(c) Peano curve   (d) Geodesic curve

18

75. Who first created the following curve?

(a) Roger Penrose   (b) S. Ramanujan
(c) Leonhard Euler   (d) William Oughtred

76. What is this curve known as ?

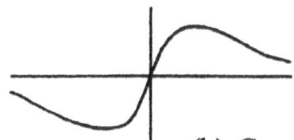

(a) Evolute   (b) Crunode
(c) Serpentine   (d) Involute

77. Which is the curve that is traced in one sweep and is closed but does not have any part retraced?
(a) Versiera   (b) Trochoid
(c) Unicursal curve   (d) Evolute

78. This curve was created by Rene Descartes. What is it called?

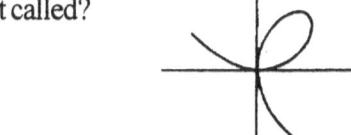

(a) Folium   (b) Hypocycloid
(c) Lituus   (d) Strophoid

79. What is this curve known as?

    (a) Pearl of Sluze   (b) Nephroid of Freeth
    (c) Cardioid   (d) Bicorn

80. Topologically, it is a simple closed curve. What is it called?

    (a) Maze   (b) Serpentine
    (c) Evolute   (d) Jordan curve

81. What is this curve known as?

    (a) Cycloid   (b) Astroid
    (c) Unicursal   (d) Hypocycloid

82. After whom is this spiral named?

    (a) G.A. Plimpton   (b) Archimedes
    (c) Jean Victor Poncelet (d) Rene Descartes

83. Which curve dominates our world more than any other?
   (a) Spiral   (b) Sine
   (c) Corkscrew   (d) Helical

84. Who invented the following spiral?

   (a) Pierre de Fermat   (b) Jacob Kobel
   (c) Isaac Newton   (d) Joseph Lagrange

85. What is this curve called?

   (a) Lotus   (b) Rose
   (c) Leaf   (d) None

86. Which curve is known as the 'Helen of geometry'?
   (a) Parabola   (b) French Curve
   (c) Ellipse   (d) Cycloid

Triangles

87. What is the point of intersection of an orthocentre?
   (a) Three bisectors of a triangle
   (b) The sides of a triangle
   (c) Three altitudes of a triangle
   (d) Two bisectors of a triangle

88. A pedal triangle is a triangle inside another figure. Which figure is it?
    (a) Circle
    (b) Cube
    (c) Ellipse
    (d) Triangle

89. What is a triangle that does not contain a right angle ?
    (a) Acute triangle
    (b) Equilateral triangle
    (c) Spherical triangle
    (d) Oblique triangle

90. For two triangles to be similar, it is enough if one of their following characteristics is correspondingly equal. Which one?
    (a) Angles
    (b) Sides
    (c) Altitudes
    (d) Areas

91. What is this figure?

    (a) Circular triangle
    (b) Spinode
    (c) Crunode
    (d) Spherical triangle

92. In any triangle ABC
    AB < BC + CA.
    What is it known as?
    (a) Triangle inequality
    (b) Bernoulli inequality
    (c) Newton's inequality
    (d) Cauchy's inequality

93. Ex-centre is the centre of a figure. Which one?
    (a) Inscribed circle   (b) Great circle
    (c) Circumscribed circle   (d) Escribed circle

94. $\sqrt{\dfrac{(s-a)(s-b)(s-c)}{s}}$ [Where a, b, c are lengths of the sides of a triangle and $s = (a+b+c)/2$] is the radius of a figure. Which one?
    (a) Inscribed circle of the triangle
    (b) Circumscribed circle of the triangle
    (c) Escribed circle of the triangle
    (d) None

95. What is this figure?

    (a) Circular triangle   (b) Cardioid
    (c) Spherical triangle   (d) Nappe

96. What is a triangle with all its sides unequal known as?
    (a) Equilateral triangle   (b) Isosceles triangle
    (c) Scalene triangle   (d) Pascal's triangle

IV

NAMING SESSION

Number Names

97. It is 12/13 of 2,3 and 4. What is it?
    - (a) Geometric mean
    - (b) Arithmetic mean
    - (c) Harmonic mean
    - (d) Heronian mean

98. What are 9, 12 and 15 together known as?
    - (a) Triangular numbers
    - (b) Triperfect numbers
    - (c) Triautomorphic numbers
    - (d) Pythagorean triples

99. What is 30 of 3, 5 and 10?
    - (a) Geometric mean
    - (b) Greatest common factor
    - (c) Lowest common multiple
    - (d) Lowest common denominator

100. What are 17 and 19, 1001 and 1003, etc., known as?
    (a) Consecutive primes
    (b) Amicable pairs
    (c) Twin primes
    (d) Sociable numbers

101. In 6387, it is 100 for 3. What is it?
    (a) Place market
    (b) Hypergeometric mean
    (c) Partial fraction   (d) Place value

102. What are prime numbers of the form $2^n - 1$ known as?
    (a) Fermat primes   (b) Mersenne primes
    (c) Hire primes   (d) Zeno primes

103. What are 3/4, 13/19, 721/859, etc., known as?
    (a) Proper fraction   (b) Simple fraction
    (c) Common fraction   (d) Vulgar fraction

104. What are the numbers 1,9,45,55,297,703,2223... known as?
    (a) Fibonacci numbers
    (b) Kaprekar numbers
    (c) Pythagoras numbers
    (d) Mersenne numbers

105. 1,2,3,4,5,6,7,8,9,0 popular as?
   (a) Hindu-Arabic numerals
   (b) Arabic numerals
   (c) Brahmi numerals   (d) Mayan numerals

106. It is 12 to 12, 60 and 84. What is it?
   (a) Lowest common multiple
   (b) Arithmetic mean
   (c) Least common denominator
   (d) Highest common factor

107. What are 1,1,2,4,7,13,24,44,81.... known as?
   (a) Carmicheal numbers (b) Lucas numbers
   (c) Fibonacci numbers   (d) Tribonacci numbers

Coining Terms

108. What is the other popular name of zero?
   (a) Cipher   (b) Naught
   (c) Null   (d) Empty

109. Who is known as the 'Adam of Mathematics' in the sense that he coined a large number of mathematical terms?
   (a) Francois Viete   (b) George Polya
   (c) Pierre-Simon Laplace
   (d) J.J. Sylvester

110. What is a decimal point sometimes called?
   (a) Mantissa   (b) Separatrix
   (c) Full point   (d) Break point

111. 'Trigon' is the old term for which word?
   (a) Trigonometry   (b) Triangle
   (c) Trihedron   (d) Trisectrix

112. 'Logarithm' has its origin in a word. Which one?
   (a) Ratio number
   (b) Artificial number
   (c) Characteristic number
   (d) Napier number

113. Who introduced the word 'focus' into the geometry of conics?
   (a) Apollonius   (b) Johann Kepler
   (c) Pappus   (d) Lazare Carnot

114. Which word comes close in Meaning to the Latin word 'axiom'?
   (a) Belief
   (b) Self-evident statement
   (c) Conditional statement
   (d) Truth

115. What is the origin of the word 'Arithmetic'?
   (a) A Greek word
   (b) The title of a book of Arabic origin
   (c) A Hindu number system
   (d) A Hebrew word

116. Who introduced 'ellipse', 'parabola' and 'hyperbola' to geometry?
   (a) Apollonius   (b) Pappus
   (c) Menelaus   (d) Claudius Ptolemy

117. What is 'casting out nines'?
   (a) A method for checking multiplication and division.
   (b) An English phrase.
   (c) A method for deleting undesirable numbers from a set.
   (d) None.

118. Who coined the term 'Artificial Intelligence' for the mathematics-based subject meant to copy human intelligence?
   (a) John McCarthy
   (b) Marvin Minowski
   (c) Alan Turing
   (d) William Shockley

119. What does the term 'postulate' mean?
    (a) An obvious and simple geometrical fact.
    (b) A geometrical truth.
    (c) A statement on geometry.
    (d) The statement that has been proved.

120. What is another mathematical name for 'Chart'?
    (a) Map   (b) Curve
    (c) Graph   (d) Section

121. The term 'algorithm'- a step by step procedure for calculation – has been derived from the name of a mathematician. Which country was he from?
    (a) India   (b) Italy
    (c) Iraq   (d) China

122. What is a square array of numbers called in which every row, column and the two diagonals add up to give the same total?
    (a) Algebraic square   (b) Euler square
    (c) Latin square   (d) Magic square

123. Who introduced the term 'Pole' to mathematics?
    (a) C.J. Brianchon
    (b) Georg Mohr
    (c) Jean Victor Poncelet
    (d) F.J. Servois

Calling By Words

124. What is a septillion?
    - (a) 10^{18}
    - (b) 10^{24}
    - (c) 10^{17}
    - (d) 10^{32}

125. What is a decade?
    - (a) 10 years
    - (b) 100 years
    - (c) 15 years
    - (d) 25 years

126. What is a trillion?
    - (a) 10^6
    - (b) 10^9
    - (c) 10^{18}
    - (d) 10^{12}

127. What is a sextillion?
    - (a) 10^{12}
    - (b) 10^{22}
    - (c) 10^{21}
    - (d) 10^{30}

128. What is a vigintillion?
    - (a) 10^{63}
    - (b) 10^{23}
    - (c) 10^{40}
    - (d) 10^{54}

129. What is a millennium?
    - (a) 10,000 years
    - (b) 100,000 years
    - (c) 1,000,000 years
    - (d) 1,000 years

130. What is a billion?
    - (a) 10^9
    - (b) 10^6
    - (c) 10^{10}
    - (d) 10^7

131. What is a quadrillion?
    (a) 10^{30} (b) 10^{11}
    (c) 10^{20} (d) 10^{15}

132. What is a quintillion?
    (a) 10^{17} (b) 10^{20}
    (c) 10^{18} (d) 10^{19}

133. What is a 'Micro'?
    (a) 10^{-6} (b) 10^{-9}
    (c) 10^{-4} (d) 10^{-8}

134. What is a 'Kilobit'?
    (a) 4^{10} (b) 10^{4}
    (c) 2^{10} (d) 10^{2}

135. Days of nano-technology are here. What is a 'Nano'?
    (a) 10^{-9} (b) 10^{-6}
    (c) 10^{-3} (d) 10^{-1}

136. What is an octillion?
    (a) 10^{20} (b) 10^{22}
    (c) 10^{27} (d) 10^{30}

Telling Prefixes

137. What is the prefix for a fraction of 10^{-15}?
    (a) Deci   (b) Centi
    (c) Femto   (d) Atto

138. 'Tetra' is the prefix for denoting a number. Which one?
   (a) Seven
   (b) Five
   (c) Four
   (d) Three

139. What is the prefix for a fraction 10^2?
   (a) Hecto   (b) Nano
   (c) Micro   (d) Milli

140. Which is the prefix denoting a fraction of 10^{-12}?
   (a) Peta   (b) Pico
   (c) Penta   (d) Hecto

141. Which is the prefix to denote 20?
   (a) Deka   (b) Penta
   (c) Icosa   (d) No prefix exists

142. Which is the prefix for 0.001?
   (a) Centi   (b) Milli
   (c) Deka   (d) Deci

143. What is the prefix for denoting eleven?
   (a) Hepta   (b) Kilo
   (c) Hexa   (d) Hendeca

144. What does the prefix 'Mega' stand for?
   (a) 1,000,000
   (b) 1,00,00
   (c) 1,00
   (d) 1,000

145. What is the prefix for a multiple of 10^9?
   (a) Hecto
   (b) Deka
   (c) Giga
   (d) None

146. What is the prefix for denoting 9?
   (a) Nano
   (b) Nona
   (c) Non
   (d) All

V

THEOREMS AND FORMULAE

Theorems

147. Which theorem is visually easy to prove but not so analytically?
    (a) Leibniz theorem
    (b) Gomory's theorem
    (c) Jordan curve theorem
    (d) Fermat's last theorem

148. 'The line joining the midpoints of two sides of a triangle is parallel to the third side and half its length.' Which is this theorem?
    (a) Menelaus' theorem
    (b) Pappus' theorem
    (c) Theorem of mean value
    (d) Midpoint theorem

149. Where does the 'correspondence theorem' figure in?
    (a) Topology   (b) Logic
    (c) Algebra   (d) Mechanics

150. What is $a^2 + b^2 = 2m^2 + 2c^2$ (where a and b are lengths of two sides of a triangle, whose third side is divided into two equal lengths c by a median of length m)?
    (a) Pappus' theorem
    (b) Theorem of mean value
    (c) Pythagoras theorem
    (d) Apollonius' theorem

151. Which theorem is jocularly put as: '...the squaw on the hippopotamus is equal to the sum of the squaws on the other two hides'?
    (a) Menelaus theorem   (b) Pythagoras theorem
    (c) Fermat's theorem   (d) Rolle's theorem

152. Any positive integer may be expressed as the sum of the squares of four integers. Which is this theorem?
    (a) Four squares theorem
    (b) Floquet theorem
    (c) Dirichlet's theorem
    (d) Lagrange's theorem

153. Which theorem states that every even number is the sum of two prime numbers?
    (a) Goldbach's theorem   (b) D'Alembert theorem
    (c) Bernoulli theorem   (d) Poisson theorem

154. $(x + a)^3 = x^3 + 3x^2a + 3xa^2 + a^3$ known as?
    (a) Ham sandwich theorem
    (b) Ratio theorem
    (c) Binomial theorem
    (d) Bernoulli theorem

155. In which subject does the 'compactness theorem' figure?
    (a) Logic   (b) Algebra
    (c) Arithmetic   (d) Trigonometry

156. Which theorem is also known as 'the Law of Large Numbers'?
    (a) Poisson theorem   (b) Bernoulli theorem
    (c) Cauchy theorem   (d) Pythagoras theorem

157. If p is prime and a is prime to p, then $a^{p-1} - 1$ is divisible by p. What is this theorem called?
    (a) Little Fermat theorem
    (b) Ptolemy's theorem
    (c) Geber's theorem
    (d) Prime Descartes theorem

Formulae

158. Who remarked, 'One cannot escape the feeling that these mathematical formulas have an inde pendent existence and an intelligence of their own, that they are wiser than their discoverers, that we get more out of them than was originally put into them'?
    (a) Heinrich Hertz
    (b) James Clerk Maxwell
    (c) Georg Cantor   (d) Albert Einstein

159. What are the following formulae?
    $(A \cup B)' = A' \cap B'$
    $(A \cap B)' = A' \cup B'$
    (where the complement of a set S is indicated by S')
    (a) Euler's formulae   (b) Stirling formulae
    (c) Wallis formulae   (d) De Morgan formulae

160. What are the formula linking temperatures in Fahrenheit (F) and Celsius (C) scale?
    (a) $F = (10/8)C + 42$ (b) $F = (9/5)C + 32$
    (c) $C = (9/5)F + 32$ (d) $C = (10/8)F + 42$

161. For what value does the formula $V + F = E + 2$ stand good (where F stands for the number of faces, E the number of edges and V the number of vertices)?
    (a) Any prism   (b) Any solid
    (c) Any polyhedron   (d) None

162. Who gave the famous formula $e^{ix} = \cos x + i \sin x$, (where $i = \sqrt{-1}$)?
  (a) Nicholas Bernoulli   (b) Leonhard Euler
  (c) Brook Taylor   (d) Colin Maclaurin

163. What does the formula $\sqrt{(x_1 - x_2)^2 + (y_1 - y_2)^2}$ represent [where (x_1, x_2) and (y_1, y_2) are two points in the Cartesian co-ordinates]?
  (a) Mean distance between the points
  (b) Distance between the points
  (c) Angle
  (d) Curve length

164. $\sin(90° + \theta) = \cos \theta$ called?
  (a) Product formula   (b) Double angle formula
  (c) Half-angle formula   (d) Reduction formula

165. What is the following formula known as?
  $c^2 = a^2 + b^2 - 2ab \cos C$ (where a, b and c are sides of a plane triangle and C the angle opposite the side c)
  (a) Cramer's rule   (b) Sine Law
  (c) Cosine Law   (d) Tangent Law

166. Who discovered the famous formula $(\cos x + i \sin x)^n = \cos nx + i \sin nx$, where $i = \sqrt{-1}$?
  (a) Johann Bernoulli   (b) Abraham De Moivre
  (c) Comte de Buffon   (d) James Stirling

167. What is 2 (l + w) [where *l* and *w* stand respectively for length and width of a rectangle] equal to?
   (a) Perimeter of the rectangle
   (b) Area of the rectangle
   (c) Diagonal of the rectangle
   (d) None of the above

168. If one has to add all the numbers from one to *n*, which formula one has to use?
   (a) $(n/2)(n + 1)$ (b) $n(n + 1)$
   (c) $(n + 1)n^2$ (d) $n(n + 1)(n + 2)$

169. What does the following formula stand for?
   $$\frac{1}{\sqrt{5}}\left[\left(\frac{1 +\sqrt{5}}{2}\right)^n - \left(\frac{1-\sqrt{5}}{2}\right)^n\right]$$
   (a) nth Lucas number
   (b) nth Mersenner number
   (c) nth Catalan number
   (d) nth Fibonacci number

170. The area of a triangle = $s(s - a)(s - b)(s - c)$
   [Where $s = (a + b + c)/2$; a, b, and c are the sides of a triangle].
   What is this formula known as?
   (a) Thales' formula   (b) Hero's formula
   (c) Euclid's formula   (d) Hesse's formula

39

171. Who discovered the formula $22\pi^4 = 2,143$ for obtaining the value of π correct up to eight decimals?

    (a) Tsu Ch'ung   (b) S. Ramanujan

    (c) William Shanks   (d) Carl F. Gauss

VI

MIND TICKLERS

Numbers

172. Which is the number that is equal to the cube of the sum of its digits?
    (a) 5,673   (b) 4,913
    (c) 5,831   (d) 5,784

173. Which is not a Fibonacci number?
    (a) 1   (b) 4
    (c) 8   (d) 21

174. What is the exact value of e, the base of natural logarithm function?
    (a) 2.7   (b) 2.73
    (c) 2.7282818   (d) None

175. Which is the first smallest amicable pair?
    (a) 220 and 284   (b) 242 and 280
    (c) 32 and 48   (d) 17,296 and 18,416

176. Which number is not a perfect number?
    (a) 28   (b) 498
    (c) 6   (d) 8128

177. Which is the number with the property
    abcd = $a^b \times c^d$?
    (a) 2592   (b) 1372
    (c) 2576   (d) 4728

178. What is the exact value of π (pi) ?
    (a) 22/7   (b) 3.14159
    (c) 3.146   (d) None

179. Which is the smallest number to be the product of
    seven prime numbers?
    (a) 362   (b) 210
    (c) 96   (d) 128

180. What is 'friendly' to the number 1,210?
    (a) 1,184   (b) 1,093
    (c) 1,105   (d) 1,111

181. Which is the first product of two odd primes?
    (a) 12   (b) 15
    (c) 18   (d) 25

182. When two is multiplied by this number the resulting number is reverse the number when two is added to it. What is that number?
    (a) 9   (b) 47
    (c) 33   (d) 20

183. What is the absolute value of −7.2 ?
    (a) 2.8   (b) 7.2
    (c) −14.8   (d) 7.0

Sum of Numbers

184. Which is the sum of factorials of numbers from one to six?
    (a) 153   (b) 145
    (c) 523   (d) 873

185. Which is the smallest number that is the sum of all the two-digit numbers made from its digits?
    (a) 132   (b) 144
    (c) 125   (d) 96

186. Which number is equal to the sum of the digits of its own cube?
    (a) 11   (b) 27
    (c) 20   (d) 2

187. Which is the smallest integer that is the sum of three squares in two ways?
    (a) 27
    (b) 18
    (c) 86
    (d) 9

188. Which is the smallest number to be the sum of two squares in two different ways?
    (a) 18   (b) 29
    (c) 40   (d) 50

189. The smaller of the two known numbers that can be written in two ways as the sum of successive powers from one onward. Which is that number?
    (a) 54   (b) 37
    (c) 31   (d) 51

190. Which is the number (other than 1 and 2) that is the sum of the factorials of its digits?
    (a) 92   (b) 246
    (c) 145   (d) 347

191. Which is the smallest cube that is the sum of three cubes?
    (a) 81   (b) 729
    (c) 216   (d) 156

192. Which is the smallest number that is the sum of three different cubes in two ways?
    (a) 621
    (b) 251
    (c) 729
    (d) 521

193. Which is the smallest number that is the sum of two squares in three different ways?
    (a) 496   (b) 99
    (c) 325   (d) 233

Number System

194. Which decimal number is equivalent to the Roman numeral C?
    (a) 50   (b) 1000
    (c) 10   (d) 100

195. What is the equivalent of 42 in the binary number system?
    (a) 101010   (b) 10111
    (c) 11001   (d) 11111

196. What is the base of the hexadecimal number system?
    (a) 6   (b) 16
    (c) 26   (d) 36

197. What is the equivalent of 600 in Roman numerals?
    (a) DC   (b) CD
    (c) M   (d) D

198. Which number is equivalent to 100,000 in binary
     notation?
    (a) 42   (b) 32
    (c) 102   (d) 44

199. What is the equivalent of 2E4 (Duodecimal number
     notation) in the decimal number system?
    (a) 526   (b) 828
    (c) 386   (d) 424

200. What is the equivalent of the Roman numeral D in
     the decimal number system?
    (a) 1000   (b) 500
    (c) 50   (d) 10

201. 10011 is a number in the binary number system. What
     is its equivalent in the decimal number system?
    (a) 21   (b) 19
    (c) 116   (d) 11

202. What is its equivalent of 2B7E (hexadecimal not-
     ation) in the decimal number system?
    (a) 2471   (b) 211714
    (c) 11101   (d) 11134

203. What is the equivalent of 500 in the octonary number system?
    (a) 1528   (b) 387
    (c) 84   (d) 764

204. What is the Roman numeral for 50?
    (a) I   (b) X
    (c) L   (d) M

205. What is the number 11 in the hexadecimal number system?
    (a) A   (b) B
    (c) C   (d) D

Magic Squares

206. What is the magic constant of a 4 × 4 magic square?
    (a) 79   (b) 34
    (c) 15   (d) 49

207. What is a magic square of the order 4 can be built up of numbers?
    (a) 3 to 18   (b) 6 to 22
    (c) 1 to 16   (d) 4 to 19

208. What is the magic constant of the smallest magic cube?
    (a) 42   (b) 65
    (c) 8   (d) None

47

209. What is the order of smallest magic square?
    (a) Four   (b) Five
    (c) Two   (d) Three

210. What is the magic constant for the smallest magic square composedly of prime numbers, including 1?
    (a) 111   (b) 217
    (c) 169   (d) 136

211. Where did the magic square originate?
    (a) China   (b) India
    (c) Peru   (d) Italy

212. What is the magic constant of a 5 × 5 magic square?
    (a) 69   (b) 65
    (c) 175   (d) 72

213. This number is associated with the smallest magic square. Which is it?
    (a) 15   (b) 34
    (c) 65   (d) 13

214. Which is the magic constant of the only possible magic hexagon?
    (a) 42   (b) 19
    (c) 144   (d) 38

215. Which is the magic constant of the smallest magic square composed of consecutive primes?
    (a) 729   (b) 5627
    (c) 4515   (d) 16,578

Figures

216. In this famous problem of 'Three squares', what can be said about angles A, B and C?

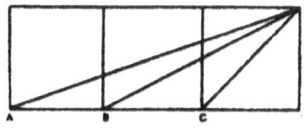

    (a) angle A + angle B = angle C
    (b) angle B + angle C = angle A
    (c) angle A + angle C = angle B
    (d) angle B = angle C

217. How many triangles are there in this diagram?

    (a) 16   (b) 20
    (c) 10   (d) 24

218. What is the interior angle of an equilateral triangle?
    (a) 57°18'   (b) 60°
    (c) 45°   (d) 30°

49

219. How many squares are there in this diagram?

   (a) 14   (b) 18
   (c) 20   (d) 8

220. Which is the polygon whose sum of its interior angles equals 900°?
   (a) Triangle   (b) Hexagon
   (c) Heptagon   (d) Icosogon

221. What is the least number of rectangles required to divide a rectangle into smaller rectangles of different shapes but equal area?
   (a) Four   (b) Six
   (c) Eighteen   (d) Seven

222. Which is the polygon whose sum of its interior angles equals 360°?
   (a) Pentagon   (b) Dodecagon
   (c) Triangle   (d) Quadrilateral

223. How many equilateral triangles are in this figure?

   (a) Four   (b) Six
   (c) Sixteen   (d) Eight

224. Which is the polygon the sum of whose interior angles equals 1440°?
  (a) Decagon
  (b) Octagon
  (c) Pentagon
  (d) Dodecagon

225. How many triangles are there in this figure?

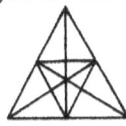

  (a) 16
  (b) 47
  (c) 50
  (d) 18

VII

SPECIALISED SUBJECTS

A Variety of Geometries

226. Who remarked, 'Geometry existed before the creation. It is co-external with the mind of God... Geometry is God itself'?
    - (a) Euclid
    - (b) Charles Hermite
    - (c) Johannes Kepler
    - (d) Rene Descartes

227. How many types of non-Euclidean geometries are there?
    - (a) Four types
    - (b) Two types
    - (c) Three types
    - (d) Eleven types

228. What is the geometry dealing with the properties of three-dimensional geometric figures known as?
    - (a) Plane geometry
    - (b) Platonic geometry
    - (c) Finite geometry
    - (d) Solid geometry

229. Which branch of geometry is concerned with the properties of figures formed on the surface of a sphere?
(a) Plane geometry
(b) Non-Euclidean geometry
(c) Projective geometry
(d) Spherical geometry

230. What is the type of geometry known as in which the sum of three angles of a triangle is greater than two right angles?
(a) Riemannian geometry
(b) Hyperbolic geometry
(c) Euclidean geometry
(d) Elinsteinian geometry

231. What is another term for "pure geometry"?
(a) Plane geometry
(b) Synthetic geometry
(c) Riemannian geometry
(d) All

232. What are the geometry and trigonometry of figures on the surface of a sphere known as?
(a) Spherical trigonometry
(b) Spherics
(c) Differential geometry
(d) None

233. Which type of geometry contains no parallel lines?
   (a) Co-ordinate geometry
   (b) Analytical geometry
   (c) Projective geometry
   (d) Solid geometry

234. What is the type of geometry known as in which the sum of three angles of a triangle is less than two right angles?
   (a) Elliptic geometry
   (b) Hyperbolic geometry
   (c) Spherical geometry
   (d) Pythagorean geometry

235. Who wrote 'Let no one destitute of geometry enter my doors' above the door of his academy?
   (a) Aryabhata   (b) Plato
   (c) Apollonius   (d) Socrates

Space

236. Who said, 'Space is not a lot of points close together; it is a lot of distances interlocked'?
   (a) A.S. Eddington
   (b) A.N. Whitehead
   (c) Bertrand Russell
   (d) Werner Heisenberg

237. In what subject are these two knots equivalent to each other?

(a) Projective geometry
(b) Analytical geometry
(c) Topology
(d) They cannot be equal in any sense

238. According to the latest theory of physics, space is most easily described as having dimensions of a particular order. Which one?
(a) Four   (b) Three
(c) Eleven   (d) Nine

239. What is this called?

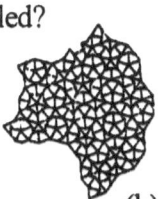

(a) Tessellation   (b) Fractuals
(c) Tiles   (d) None

240. What are infinite-dimensional forms called?
(a) Hyperspaces   (b) Hilbert spaces
(c) Strings   (d) Infinite spaces

241. What is this figure known as?

   (a) Mandelbrot's figure   (b) Koch's island
   (c) Fractual   (d) Hexagram

242. What is name of this thing?

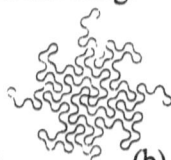

   (a) Tetrahexes   (b) Dragon curve
   (c) Tessellation   (d) Koch's curve

243. What is a 'Hyperspace'?
   (a) A multi-dimensional space
   (b) A curved three-dimensional space
   (c) An infinite-dimensional space
   (d) Something beyond space

244. What is this graphical way of representing a
problem?

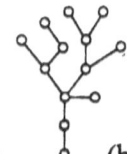

   (a) Tree diagram   (b) Feynman diagram
   (c) Forest diagram   (d) Branch diagram

245. What is this beetle-shaped figure?

(a) Julia set   (b) Fatou dust
(c) Siegel disc   (d) Mandelbrot set

Statistics

246. What is an experiment in which there are two possible outcomes known as?
   (a) Random selection   (b) Bernoulli trial
   (c) Simple random sampling
   (d) Tally

247. What is the ratio of the probability of an event occurring to that of its not occurring called?
   (a) Outcome   (b) Odds
   (c) Percentile   (d) Ordinal number

248. An impossible event is one whose probability of occurrence is this number. Which one?
   (a) Ten   (b) One
   (c) Zero   (d) Four

249. Who said, 'God does not play dice'?
   (a) Bertrand Russell   (b) P.A.M. Dirac
   (c) A.N. Whitehead   (d) Albert Elinstein

250. What is the curve illustrated below called?

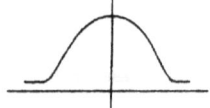

    (a) Laplacian curve   (b) Normal curve

    (c) Sine curve   (d) Cosine curve

251. What is the way in which a statistical experiment is planned known as?
    (a) Experimental design   (b) Lattice diagram
    (c) Latin square
    (d) Factorial experiment

252. What is the action of turning the TV on and off mathematically known as?
    (a) Supplementary event
    (b) Complementary event
    (c) Adjoining event
    (d) Adjacent event

253. The origin of the subject of probability is attributed to a single problem. What is it called?
    (a) Problem of the points
    (b) Problem of the stakes
    (c) The gambler's problem
    (d) None

254. Who remarked, 'Natural selection is a mechanism for generation an exceedingly high degree of improbability'?
(a) Charles Darwin   (b) Stephen Jay Gould
(c) R.A. Fisher   (d) Paul Ehrlich

255. Which philosopher said, 'Probability is the very guide of life'?
(a) Aristotle   (b) Plato
(c) Cicero   (d) Socrates

256. What is this way of presenting facts and figures?

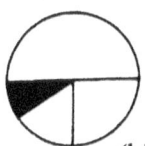

(a) Histogram   (b) Bar chart
(c) Pictogram   (d) Pie chart

257. Who started in 1950 the National Sample Survey with the aim to collect all types of data on the populace of India?
(a) T.T. Krichnamachari (b) M.N. Saha
(c) C.R. Rao   (d) P.C. Mahalanobis

VIII

PORTRAIT QUIZ

258. Who is this king-like mathematician? He is the inventor of the logarithm.

259. This curly long-haired mathematician is the founder of coordinate geometry. Who is he?

260. This mathematician developed the concept of elliptic functions. Who is he?

261. This goatee-sporting mathematician is the founder of 'Cybernetics'. Who is he?

262. This casual photo of an electronic engineer is the inventor of the first electronic computer built on his kitchen table. Who is he?

263. This cap-wearing mathematician applied mathematics to electricity and magnetism, apart from making pioneering contributions to the subject. Who is he?

264. Although he must have never seen a calculator in his life-time, his mathematical work is the foundation of the present computer. Who is he?

265. Who is this Congress-cap clad Indian mathematician?

266. A computer pioneer, he gave the basic theory of a computing device. Who is he?

267. He is a philosopher of mathematics. Who is he?

268. This bearded mathematician has made important contributions to non-Euclidean geometry. Who is he?

269. A mathematician who also wrote novels. Who is she?

270. A multi-faceted personality, he independently invented calculus in Europe.

271. A computer pioneer, he built the world's first programme-controlled calculator Harvard Mark I. Who is he?

272. This smiling Indian computer scientist has made important contributions to artificial intelligence and robotics. Who is he?

IX

INSTRUMENTS AND MACHINES

Instruments

273. Which is the instrument used for drawing large circles?
    - (a) Pantograph
    - (b) Beam compass
    - (c) Straight-edge
    - (d) Bow compass

274. Which device is used for measuring the area of an irregular plane figure?
    - (a) Callipers
    - (b) Bow compass
    - (c) Planimeter
    - (d) Theodolite

275. Which is the instrument that measures angles, sideways or up and down, for making maps?
    - (a) Sextant
    - (b) Beam compass
    - (c) Theodolite
    - (d) Spirit level

276. Which device is used only for multiplying and dividing numbers?
   (a) Slide rule
   (b) Divider
   (c) Mechanical calculator
   (d) Computer

277. Which is the instrument commonly used for measuring angles?
   (a) Planimeter
   (b) Protractor
   (c) Bow compass
   (d) French curve

278. Which is the instrument used for measuring the angle of the sun above the horizon?
   (a) Telescope
   (b) Callipers
   (c) Pantograph
   (d) Sextant

279. What is Napier's bones used for?
   (a) For calculating logarithm tables.
   (b) For multiplying, divide, and taking square roots of numbers.
   (c) For drawing an ellipse.
   (d) For drawing geometrical figures.

280. Which is the instrument used for drawing straight lines?
   (a) Theodolite
   (b) Ruler
   (c) Straight-edge
   (d) French curve

281. Which instrument is used for measuring the curvature of a surface?
    (a) Vernier calliper   (b) Micrometer
    (c) Inclinometer   (d) Spherometer

282. Which is believed to be the most ancient device used for calculation purposes?
    (a) Abacus   (b) Napier bones
    (c) Slide rule   (d) Calculating clock

283. What is the instrument used to measure the angle a star makes with the horizon?
    (a) Sextant   (b) Astrolabe
    (c) Spectroscope   (d) Telescope

284. Which is the mechanical device used for determining areas under curves?
    (a) Pantograph   (b) Planimeter
    (c) Integraph   (d) Hodograph

Machines

285. Who build the first 'logic machine' which could solve roblems in format logic?
    (a) John Venn   (b) Ramon Lull
    (c) Charles Stanhope   (d) Charles Babbage

286. Which is the calculating machine that caught the imagination of the public and convinced it of the arrival of an 'electronic brain'?
   (a) Harvard Mark I   (b) ENIAC
   (c) MANIAC   (d) Apple II

287. He built the first workable 'logic machine' which could solve a problem faster than a human being. Who is he?
   (a) William Stanley Jevons
   (b) Claude Shannon
   (c) Allan Marquand   (d) Arthur Samuel

288. Which is the first code-breaking machine?
   (a) Harvard Mark II   (b) Colossus
   (c) Millionaire   (d) ILLIAC

289. What is the purpose of this machine?

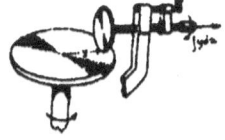

   (a) To solve problems in group theory
   (b) To draw geometrical figures
   (c) To solve differential equations
   (d) None

290. Who built the first calculating machine that solved differential equations?
(a) William S. Burroughs
(b) James Thomson
(c) Howard H. Aiken (d) Vannevar Bush

291. It is an imaginary yet profound machine composed simply of a tape and a scanner. What is it?
(a) Turing machine (b) Newcomen engine
(c) Watt engine (d) Analytical engine

292. Which is the device popular from the time of ancient Egypt for generating random numbers?
(a) Abacus (b) Mark I
(c) Roulette (d) Cubical dice

293. Which game did a 'thinking' machine play for the first time?
(a) Chess (b) Ludo
(c) Bridge (d) Carrom

294. What is the name of the 'thinking machine' which defeated the chess Grandmaster Gary Kasparov?
(a) Godhead (b) Eliza
(c) Deep Blue (d) Arnold

X

APPLICATIONS OF MATHEMATICS

Famous Problems in Science

295. An ancient Greek mathematician made an almost exact estimate of an aspect of a heavenly body using simple observations and calculations. What is it?
    (a) The radius of the Moon.
    (b) The diameter of the Sun.
    (c) The circumference of the Earth.
    (d) The mass of the Moon.

296. Someone did a simple mathematical calculation and forwarded a revolutionary biological theory. What was that theory?
    (a) The theory of evolution of life.
    (b) The theory of circulation of blood.
    (c) The germ theory of diseases.
    (d) The theory of co-evolution.

297. Who mathematically predicted the presence of the planet Neptune?
   (a) John Couch Adams (b) William Herschel
   (c) Urban Jean Leverrier (d) George Airy

298. Which heavenly body appeared – soon after it was discovered and then lost – at the precise position predicted by mathematical tools?
   (a) Uranus   (b) Ceres
   (c) Neptune   (d) Charon

299. Dmitri Mendeelev found that every eighth element had chemical properties similar to the first one of that set, if the known elements are arranged in the order of their atomic weights. These numbers led him to discover and predict the properties of three new elements. What were those elements?
   (a) Californium, Fermium, and Gallium
   (b) Hafnium, Einsteinium, and Holmium
   (c) Iridium, Chromium, and Berkelium
   (d) Scandium, Gallium, and Germanium

300. $a = 0.4 + 0.3 \times 2^n$, where n = infinity, 0, 1, 2.....
   This is a famous yet puzzling law in astronomy. What does a stand for?
   (a) The mean distance to the Sun
   (b) The size of the Sun
   (c) The mean distance to the Earth
   (d) One astronomical unit

301. Who gave the four key laws of electro-magnetism in precise mathematical form?
   (a) James Clerk Maxwell
   (b) Michael Faraday
   (c) Joseph Henry
   (d) Heinrich Hertz

302. 'Epicycles' were used to explain the orbits of planets and the Sun around the Earth in a theory of the universe. Who gave this theory?
   (a) Claudius Ptolemy   (b) Nicolaus Copernicus
   (c) Aristotle   (d) Hipparchus

303. The property of a mathematical curve was used to produce a perfect pendulum. Which is that curve?
   (a) Cycloid   (b) Helix
   (c) Ellipse   (d) Parabola

304. Who first conducted a mathematical study of the motion of an object on a spring?
   (a) Isaac Newton   (b) Isaac Barrow
   (c) Christian Huygens   (d) Robert Hooke

305. Who examined for the first time in a mathematical manner the motion of a body on an inclined plane?
   (a) Francis Bacon   (b) Galileo Galilei
   (c) Roger Bacon   (d) Christian Huygens

306. Which revolutionary idea came from simple arithmetical calculation that atomic weights of elements are multiples of that of hydrogen?
(a) Binding energy.
(b) The building block is one.
(c) Isotopes exist.
(d) Elements follow the Periodic law.

307. Who introduced 'ellipse' as the shape of orbits of planets around the Sun?
(a) Nicolaus Corpernicus
(b) Tycho Brahe
(c) Galileo Galilei
(d) Johannes Kepler

308. The Greek engineer Hero once showed his compatriots how to dig a tunnel under a mountain by starting at both ends at once. Which subject did he use to estimate the points where digging could be started simultaneously?
(a) Calculus
(b) Geometry
(c) Arithmetic
(d) Trigonometry

309. Which is the industry in which the phrase 'the tyranny of numbers' had once become popular and led to a marvellous invention?
(a) Chemical industry
(b) Electronics industry
(c) Oil industry
(d) Book industry

Applied Mathematics

310. What kind of geometrical reflecting surface would concentrate parallel rays to one point?
    (a) Paraboloid   (b) Cycloid
    (c) Hypocycloid   (d) Hyperboloid

311. What is the astronomical term 'azimuth' associated with?
    (a) Spherical co-ordinates
    (b) Cylindrical co-ordinates
    (c) Polar co-ordinates
    (d) Curvilinear co-ordinates

312. As mathematical formulae are approximations, how does an engineer, for instance, design steel beams for bridges so that they do not collapse when built?
    (a) He makes beams far stronger than what the formula dictates.
    (b) He makes the beams far weaker than what the formula dictates.
    (c) He does not care for approximation.
    (d) He does not care for formula.

313. When parallel rays are coming from an object, it is supposed to be lying at this. What is it?
    (a) Zero   (b) A great distance
    (c) Infinity   (d) A nearby place

314. Which phenomenon was first explained using Fourier analysis?
    (a) A rocket flight.
    (b) Motion of vibrating string.
    (c) Motion of a vibrating tuning fork.
    (d) Sound waves.

315. $d^2x/dt^2 = -K^2x$
    (where K is a constant and x the distance traveled by a particle in time t)
    What does the above equation represent?
    (a) Linear motion of the particle
    (b) Simple harmonic motion of the particle
    (c) Accelerated motion of the particle
    (d) Frictionless motion of the particle

316. Which mathematician's statistical methods have been used in agriculture?
    (a) R. A. Fisher   (b) M. J. Moroney
    (c) Edmund Halley   (d) L. C. Tippett

317. $dN/dt = KN$
    (where K is a constant, t the time and N the number of bacteria present). What is it?
    (a) The law of bacterial growth
    (b) The law of bacterial population
    (c) The law of organic growth
    (d) The law of bacterial decay

318. Which curve is of special importance in electronics?
    (a) Jordan curve
    (b) Dragon curve
    (c) Cassinian curve
    (d) Bowditch curve

319. What is the following differential equation known as?
    L (dI/dt) + RI = E
    (where I is current in a circuit that has R resistance and L inductance, and E the external electromotive force).
    (a) Helmholtz equation
    (b) Maxwell's equation
    (c) Lorentz equation
    (d) Coulomb's equation

320. Mathematical study of oscillatory motion began with the basic aim to improve the method of this. What is it?
    (a) Assessing the properties of oscillating bodies.
    (b) Telling time.
    (c) Ascertaining the elasticity of strings or springs.
    (d) Determining the movement of planets.

321. What is the centre of mass of a body called?
    (a) Circumcentre   (b) Radical centre
    (c) Barycentre   (d) Centroid

322. For building his 'geodesics' – dome-shaped surfaces – Buckminster Fuller used one common geometrical shape in thousands. Which one?
(a) Equilateral triangle
(b) Hexagon
(c) Pentagon
(d) Square

In Term of Mathematics

323. What does (mass × acceleration due to gravity × height) stand for?
(a) Potential energy   (b) Kinetic energy
(c) Momentum   (d) Angular momentum

324. F = 2mwv
(where w is the angular velocity of the rotation of the Earth, v is the speed of the object of mass m relative to the Earth).
What is F?
(a) Centrifugal force   (b) Centripetal force
(c) Coriolis force   (d) Gravity

325. Which common word has today become an important mathematical concept?
(a) Error   (b) Magnitude
(c) Size   (d) Chance

326. At a given temperature, P × V = constant (where P is pressure and V volume of a gas). What is this law called?
    (a) Charles's law   (b) Boyle's law
    (c) Pascal's law   (d) Lenz's law

327. What does $\sqrt{2GM/r}$ stand for? (where M is the mass of a planet, G gravitational constant, and r the radius of the planet)
    (a) Gravitational force   (b) Coriolis force
    (c) Escape velocity   (d) Projectile velocity

328. What does $gt^2/2$ stand for, when g is the acceleration due to gravity and t time?
    (a) Gravitational constant.
    (b) The altitude to which a body rises or falls from in t time.
    (c) The distance covered by a vehicle in t time.
    (d) The speed with which a body rises up or falls down.

329. What does 2pi/period $\left(\dfrac{2\pi}{t}\right)$ represent in the physical sense?
    (a) Angular frequency
    (b) Angular momentum
    (c) Centripetal force
    (d) Centrifugal force

330. What does pi × radius²/height $\left(\dfrac{\pi r^2}{h}\right)$ represent physically ?

    (a) Volume of a cone.

    (b) Volume of a right circular cylinder.

    (c) Area of a tetrahedron.

    (d) Mass of a cuboid.

331. What does (C – 2.5 log I) stand for, if I is light intensity and C a constant determined by the unit with which I is measured ?

    (a) Apparent magnitude of a star

    (b) Absolute brightness of a luminous object

    (c) Standard brightness

    (d) Visual brightness of a distant object

332. What does $(-\log [H_3 O^+])$ stand for, if H_2O^+ is concentration of hydrogen ions?

    (a) Acidity of a solution.

    (b) Polarity of hydrogen concentration.

    (c) Alkalinity of a solution.

    (d) Concentration of hydrogen.

333. What are Gregor Mendel's laws of heredity based on?

    (a) Probability theory   (b) Topological theory

    (c) Fibonacci numbers   (d) Symbolic logic

334. What is velocity – but not speed?

    (a) Scalar quantity   (b) Vector quantity

    (c) Variable quantity   (d) Constant quantity

XI

MATHEMATICS AFFECTS HUMANITIES

Literature

335. Which writer resorted to algebraic symbols to
     impart clarity to his humorous writings?
     (a) George Mikes   (b) Miguel de Cervantes
     (c) Jerome K. Jerome   (d) Jonathan Swift

336. Which story gives an idea about statistics?
     (a) *Inflexible Logic*
     (b) *Geometry in the South Pacific*
     (c) *Young Archimedes*
     (d) *Cycloid Pudding*

337. Which number runs throughout William
     Shakespeare's *The Merchant of Venice*?
     (a) Four   (b) Six
     (c) Nine   (d) Three

338. Arthur Koestler's *Roots of Coincidence* is an interesting collection of anecdotes centred on this mathematical concept. What is it?
    (a) Zero   (b) Random numbers
    (c) Series   (d) Chance

339. Which classic contains references to numbers whose significance is still being dug out by mathematicians?
    (a) *Island of Laputa*
    (b) *The Republic*
    (c) *Looking Glass Universe*
    (d) *Flatland*

340. Who is the author of the geometry-oriented science fiction *Flatland*?
    (a) Philip J. Davis   (b) Peter B. Scott
    (c) Edwin A. Abbot   (d) Brain Ball

341. Which classic contains a section on mathematics?
    (a) *Lord of the Flies*   (b) *The Plague*
    (c) *Finnegans Wake*   (d) *The Castle*

342. 'The world can be made intelligent in terms of right angles'. This statement was made in a world famous classic. Which is that classic?
    (a) *The Timaeus*   (b) *The Odyssey*
    (c) *The Wasps*   (d) *The Rubaiyat*

343. Which is the science fiction in which a group of children stumble upon a toy abacus from a four-dimensional world which teaches them how to think four-dimensionally?
   (a) *ET*
   (b) *Mimsy Were the Borogoves*
   (c) *The Wizard of Oz*
   (d) *Islands in the Sky*

344. What has novelist Lawrence Sterne's *Tristram Shandy* contributed to the world of mathematics?
   (a) A paradox   (b) A theorem
   (c) A formula
   (d) A mathematical symbol

345. Which story shows how the law of averages fail?
   (a) *Surreal Numbers*
   (b) *No-Sided Professor*
   (c) *The Law*
   (d) *The Wall of Darkness*

346. Which book on mathematics has been described as 'a scientific poem'?
   (a) *Mecanique Anaytique*
   (b) *Mecanique Celeste*
   (c) *Mysterium Cosmographicum*
   (d) *Arithmetica Universalis*

347. Who narrates his experiences in a one-dimensional
world as depicted in the classic science fiction
Flatland?
    (a) A Triangle   (b) A Circle
    (c) A Square   (d) A Rectangle

Art and Music

348. Which famous artist's painting had the strongest
mathematical appeal in recent years?
    (a) Pablo Picasso   (b) Salvador Dali
    (c) M.C. Escher   (d) Joseph Beuys

349. 'The senses delight in things duly proportional'. Who
made this statement relating beauty to mathematics?
    (a) Leonardo da Vinci   (b) Thomas Aquinas
    (c) Georges Seurat   (d) Piet Mondrian

350. Which is the engraving/ painting in which a magic
square is depicted?
    (a) Annunciation   (b) Melancholia
    (c) Resurrection   (d) Last Supper

351. Whose paintings contain fantastic tassellations which
depict aspects of symmetry, group theory, and
crystallographic laws?
    (a) Leonardo da Vinci   (b) Pablo Picasso
    (c) M.C. Escher   (d) Salvador Dali

352. Which branch of mathematics was born out of painting?
   (a) Topology   (b) Projective geometry
   (c) Solid geometry   (d) None

353. 'Through and through the world is infested with quantity: To talk sense is to talk quantities... You may fly to poetry and music, and quantity and number will face you in your rhythms and your octaves'. Who said these words?
   (a) James Jeans   (b) A.N.Whitehead
   (c) Samuel Pepys   (d) W.W. Rouse Ball

354. Which artist made the pioneering effort to incorporate three-dimensionality in his paintings?
   (a) Leonardo da Vinci   (b) Giotto
   (c) Uccello   (d) Mantegna

355. Who showed first that all sounds, musical or otherwise, are completely describable in mathematical terms?
   (a) Simeon Poisson   (b) C.V. Raman
   (c) Joseph Fourier   (d) J.S.Bach

356. Which cartoonist often turns mathematical symbols into humorous human relations?
   (a) R.K. Laxman   (b) Ronald Searle
   (c) Edward Sorel   (d) Saul Steinberg

357. An artist as well as a mathematician, he wrote a book on geometrical constructions and perspective meant for artists. Who was he?
    (a) Botticelli   (b) Duccio
    (c) Albrecht Durer   (d) Vasari

358. Who said, 'Music is the pleasure the human soul experiences from counting without being aware that it is counting'?
    (a) Charles Lamb   (b) G.W. Leibniz
    (c) Joseph Lagrange   (d) William Blake

359. Which architect felt that mathematics has made human life comfortable?
    (a) Charles Correa   (b) Buckminster Fuller
    (c) Frank Lloyd Wright (d) Le Corbusier

360. Which artist wrote, 'Let no one who is not a mathematician read my works'?
    (a) Frans Hals   (b) Magritte
    (c) Rubens   (d) Leonardo da Vinci

Philosophy

361. What is the foundation of mathematics viewed through?
    (a) Four standard isms
    (b) Three standard dogmas
    (c) Two basic tenets   (d) None

362. Who forwarded in his book this motto : 'The purpose of computing is insight, not numbers'?
   (a) Richard W. Hamming
   (b) Bertrand Russell
   (c) Joseph Needham
   (d) E. T. Bell

363. Who founded the Intuitionist School of Mathematics?
   (a) A.N. Whitehead   (b) John von Neumann
   (c) Georg Canter   (d) L.E.J. Brouwer

364. 'The only entities that may be admitted to mathematics are those that are constructible, and only those propositions may be entertained whose truth can be proved in a finite number of steps'. What is this philosophy of mathematics called?
   (a) Platonism   (b) Finitism
   (b) Constructivism   (d) Formalism

365. The emergence of a subject led to drastic changes in the ethical, moral, and religious value. Which is that subject?
   (a) Statistics   (b) Number theory
   (c) Non-Euclidean geometry
   (d) Calculus of variation

366. Who is the founding father of the Formalist School of Mathematics?
    (a) Kurt Godel
    (b) Bertrand Russell
    (c) David Hilbert
    (d) G. W. Leibniz

367. Who said, 'The new power is not money in the hands of the few, but information in the hands of the many'?
    (a) Claude Shannon
    (b) Norbert Wiener
    (c) John Naisbitt
    (d) Marvin Minsky

368. Who founded the Logistic School of Mathematics?
    (a) G.W. Leibniz
    (b) Bertrand Russell
    (c) A.N. Whitehead
    (d) George Boole

369. Who argued that '…the man ignorant of mathematics will be increasingly limited in his grasp of the main forces of civilization'?
    (a) Claude Shannon
    (b) Kurt Godel
    (c) John Kemeny
    (d) Richard Bellman

370. Himself an esteemed philosopher of mathematics, he wrote solely and extensively on the philosophy of mathematics. Who is he?
    (a) Garrett Birkhoff
    (b) Ludwig Wittgenstein
    (c) Bertrand Russell
    (d) John von Neumann

371. Which philosopher of mathematics said, 'There can never be surprises in logic'?
    (a) Imre Lakatos   (b) Bertrand Russell
    (c) Ludwig Wittgenstein (d) Richard Dedekind

372. Who speculated that the presence of the infinite in mathematics runs parallel to religious intuition?
    (a) A.N. Whitehead   (b) Hermann Weyl
    (c) A.S. Eddington   (d) James Jeans

373. 'Mathematical entities do not exist independently of our construction of them.' What is this philosophy of mathematics called?
    (a) Intuitionism   (b) Platonism
    (c) Constructivism   (d) None

374. Which mathematician believes that the purpose of mathematics is to reveal a supreme religious goal for mankind?
    (a) I.R. Shafarevitch   (b) Alan Turing
    (c) Werner Heisenberg   (d) Bertrand Russell

375. 'Mathematical entities have a real existence independent of our conception of them'. What is this mathematical philosophy called?
    (a) Logicism   (b) Formalism
    (c) Realism   (d) Nothing

XII

MATHEMATICS AND HISTORY

Number in Ancient Times

376. What did the ancient Babylonians base their number system on?
    (a) 20   (b) 10
    (c) 6   (d) 60

377. Which number system was commonly used in various ancient civilisations and is used even today in some regions?
    (a) Twelve   (b) Five
    (c) Ten   (d) Four

378. Where do the symbols below represent numbers?
    (a) Babylonian Cuneiform
    (b) Attic Greek numeral system
    (c) Egyptian hieroglyphics   ᕴ. ᒥ. ᕒ. ᕲ.
    (d) Chinese-Japanese numeral system

379. Which civilisation first used dot patterns to represent numbers?
- (a) Chinese
- (b) Inca
- (c) Babylonian
- (d) Indus

380. Where have the earliest examples of the present numeral system been found?
- (a) In a cave near Pune
- (b) In a cave near Nasik
- (c) On the Asoka Pillar at Patna
- (d) On the seals at Mohenjo-daro

381. Where do $\in \sigma$, ψ, μ etc., belong?
- (a) Greek numeral system
- (b) Brahmi numeral system
- (c) Coptic numeral system
- (d) Arabic numeral system

382. Where were numbers represented by words for the first time?
- (a) Mayan civilisation
- (b) Babylonian civilisation
- (c) Greek civilisation
- (d) Indian civilisation

383. Which numbers are ancient in origin?
- (a) Fibonacci numbers
- (b) Kaprekar numbers
- (c) Mersenne numbers
- (d) Figurate numbers

384. What are X, M, V, L, etc.?
- (a) Arabic numerals
- (b) Roman numerals
- (c) Greek numerals
- (d) Moorish numerals

385. Where were odd numbers denoted as males and the even numbers as females?
- (a) Babylonian civilisation
- (b) Chinese civilisation
- (c) Indian civilisation
- (d) Mayan civilisation

386. Apart from number system, zero, and negative numbers, ancient Indians are held in high esteem for their contributions to this field. What is it?
- (a) Indeterminate equations
- (b) Conic section
- (c) Trigonometric series
- (d) Calculus of variations

History

387. Where did the 'galley' method of long division, which was popular before 1600, originate in?
- (a) Egypt
- (b) China
- (c) India
- (d) Greece

388. What were ancient Indians – otherwise adept at calculations – not good at?
- (a) Geometry
- (b) Presentation
- (c) Mensuration
- (d) Statistics

389. Who is the founder of the cult that claimed that 'the essence of all things is number'?
    (a) Archimedes   (b) Pythagoras
    (c) Euclid   (d) Brahmagupta

390. Which mathematician contemplated the creation of a universal language, 'Characterstica universalis', and a precise science of reasoning, 'Calculus ratiocinator'?
    (a) G.W. Leibniz   (b) A.N. Whitehead
    (c) Leonardo Fibonacci (d) J.D.H. Donnay

391. Which ancient civilisation did not feel the need for zero?
    (a) Indian   (b) Mayan
    (c) Babylonian   (d) Greek

392. What does Babylonian geometry mainly solve?
    (a) Algebraic equations
    (b) Trigonometric equations
    (c) Arithmetic calculations
    (d) Triangular problems

393. Zephirum, Iziphra, Cenero and Sifr are different names of this number. Which one?
    (a) Infinity   (b) Zero
    (c) Ten   (d) One hundred

394. Which natural phenomenon was used in ancient times to estimate the height of an object?
   (a) Rising and setting of stars.
   (b) Motion of the Moon.
   (c) Shadows cast by the Sun.
   (d) River floods.

395. What is the Bakhshali manuscript, which gives an idea of mathematics in ancient India, named after?
   (a) The person who discovered it
   (b) The monastery where it was found
   (c) The village where it was found
   (d) The village God where it was found

396. What are the pyramids of Egypt monuments to truths about?
   (a) Squares   (b) Triangles
   (c) Tetrahedrons   (d) Lines

397. It is claimed that the priest architects of Egypt could lay out a right angle with the aid of a rope divided into one ratio by three knots. Which one?
   (a) 3 : 4 : 5   (b) 6 : 8 : 27
   (c) 4 : 8 : 16   (d) 2 : 3 : 4

398. Who wrote an elaborate history of Greek geometry from its earliest origins?
   (a) Philolaus   (b) Eudemus
   (c) Proclus   (d) Thales

399. Which ancient book contains 64 Hexagrams?
    (a) *Elements*   (b) *Rhind Papyrus*
    (c) *Surya-Siddhanta*
    (d) *The Book of Changes*

400. One of the following mathematicians prepared the trigonometric tables seen in modern textbooks. Who is he?
    (a) Leonardo Fibonacci (b) Claudius Prolemy
    (c) Eudoxus   (d) John Napier

401. Which ancient mathematician set up a secret society whose emblem was a geometrical five star figure?
    (a) Euclid   (b) Brahmagupta
    (c) Pythagoras   (d) Archimedes

402. Whose motto was 'A figure and a platform, not a figure and six pence'?
    (a) Ancient Hindu mathematicians.
    (b) Ancient Greek mathematicians.
    (c) Medieval Arab mathematicians.
    (d) Ancient Egyptian mathematicians.

403. Where did the most popular method of long multiplication 'Gelosia' in the 15th and 16th century world originate?
    (a) India   (b) China
    (c) Greece   (d) South America

404. Who wrote one of the oldest documents on mathematics, *Rhind Papyrus*?
    (a) Ahmose   (b) Imhotep
    (c) Thales   (d) Anonymous

Archaeology

405. Which is the most remarkable Babylonian mathematical tablet?
    (a) Plimpton 22   (b) Plimpton 322
    (c) Plimpton 432   (d) None

406. This bundle of knots, 'Quipu', was used to keep a record of numbers. Where in the world was this practice of keeping numbers found?

    (a) China   (b) Peru
    (c) Hawaii   (d) Egypt

407. Where were red-and black-coloured rods used to denote positive and negative numbers respectively?
    (a) Babylonia   (b) Peru
    (c) China   (d) India

408. What does this ancient Indian altar 'Vakrapakshayenachit' built for some religious rituals indicate?

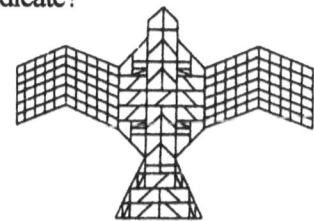

(a) The shapes of bricks used in the structure.
(b) The knowledge of geometry of its builder.
(c) The knowledge of mensuration of its builder.
(d) The diverse variety of the bricks used in the structure.

409. Where has an ivory scale of linear measurement of the time of the Indus Valley civilisation been found ?
(a) Mohenjo-daro   (b) Harappa
(c) Lothal   (d) Kalibangan

410. What was the Antikythera device found in an ancient shipwreck off a Greek island?
(a) An analog computer
(b) A digital computer
(c) A slide-rule
(d) None

411. What is remarkable about the famous *Rhind Papyrus* of Egypt?
  (a) It is about six metres long and one-third metre broad.
  (b) It is written by a mathematician.
  (c) It contains 20 solved mathematical problems.
  (d) It is a mathematical text in the form of a practical handbook.

412. In the Stonehenge, the primitive astronomical observatory, in what form are the stones arranged?
  (a) Rectangle   (b) Square
  (c) Circle   (d) Triangle

413. What does this ancient diagram represent?

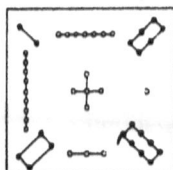

  (a) Quadrangle   (b) Number game
  (c) Multifoil   (d) Magic square

Historic Dates

414. When was *Rhind Papyrus*, the oldest document on mathematics, discovered?
  (a) 1768   (b) 1912
  (c) 1777   (d) 1858

415. When was the 'Four-colour conjecture' – every map on a flat surface or a sphere can be coloured without using more than four different colours – proved?
    (a) 1897   (b) 1976
    (c) 1980   (d) 1890

416. When was the famous Fermat's Last Theorem proved conclusively?
    (a) 1789   (b) 1987
    (c) 1850   (d) None

417. When did Leonardo Fibonacci's *Liber Abaci*, which introduced Indian numbers, including zero, to Europe, appear?
    (a) 1202   (b) 1808
    (c) 1345   (d) 1109

418. When did the first printed book on mathematics appear?
    (a) 1562   (b) 1478
    (c) 1627   (d) 1703

419. When did Kurt Godel give his famous Incompleteness Theorem?
    (a) 1931   (b) 1982
    (c) 1956   (d) 1960

420. When was International Business Machine (IBM), the pioneer computer company, set up?
    (a) 1804   (b) 1927
    (c) 1947   (d) 1914

421. When was the Linux computer operating system developed?
    (a) 1991   (b) 1981
    (c) 2001   (d) 1971

422. When did Wilhelm Schickardt build the first calculating machine or computer, called 'Calculating Clock'?
    (a) 1623   (b) 1783
    (c) 1863   (d) 1903

423. When was the Microsoft Corporation – the pioneering computer software company – set up?
    (a) 1955   (b) 1965
    (c) 1975   (d) 1985

XIII

MATHEMATICS AND INDIA

History and People

424. 'A mixture of pearl shells and sour dates...of costly crystals and common pebbles,' said a noted writer and traveller about mathematics in India. Who was he?
    (a) Marco Polo   (b) Al-Beruni
    (c) Gerbert   (d) Hiuen Tsang

425. Which ancient Greek mathematician had visited India?
    (a) Eudoxus   (b) Pythagoras
    (c) Conon   (d) Apollonius

426. Which is the earliest document on geometry of the ancient Indians?
    (a) *Taittiriya-samhita*   (b) *Sulva-sutras*
    (c) *Mimamsa-sutra*
    (d) *Baudhayana sulva-sutras*

427. Who wrote the mathematical classic *Aryabhatiya*?
    (a) Aryabhata II
    (b) Bhaskara I
    (c) Bhaskara II
    (d) Aryabhata I

428. What contains comprehensive compilation of administrative statistics?
    (a) *Arthasastra*
    (b) *Nitisastra*
    (c) *Varttika*
    (d) *Ain-i-Akbari*

429. Who is the first Indian recognised for making contribution to modern mathematics?
    (a) S. Ramanujan
    (b) Ram Chandra
    (c) B.C. Mukherjee
    (d) N.D. Rajan

430. Which Indian king ordered the translation of Euclid's *Elements* into Sanskrit?
    (a) Prithviraj Chauhan
    (b) Sawai Jai Singh II
    (c) Rana Pratap
    (d) Shahjahan

431. What were the Jaina mathematicians fond of?
    (a) Drawing geometrical curves.
    (b) Enumerating large numbers.
    (c) Drawing geometrical figures.
    (d) All.

432. The science historian George Sarton describes this ancient Indian mathematician as 'one of the greatest scientists of his race and the greatest of his time'. Who is he?

(a) Aryabhata I   (b) Mahavira

(c) Narayana   (d) Brahmagupta

433. *Sind Hind*, a classic on astronomy and mathematics, was popular in the Arab world. What text was it originally?

(a) *Khandakhadyaka*

(b) *Brahmasphuta – siddhanta*

(c) *Mahasiddhanta*

(d) *Bija-ganita*

434. Under which Indian king's reign Bhaskara's *Leelavati* was translated into Persian?

(a) Aurangzeb   (b) Shivaji

(c) Akbar   (d) Humayun

435. Who was the first scientist to apply statistical methods to predict the onset of monsoon in India?

(a) S.K. Banerji

(b) Gilbert Walker

(c) S.R. Savur

(d) C.W.B. Normand

436. When was the Indian Statistical Institute established?
   (a) 1931 (b) 1945
   (c) 1952 (d) 1960

437. Which Indian mathematician came close to inventing differential calculus?
   (a) Mahavira (b) Sridhara
   (c) Bhaskara (d) Sripati

438. His statistical techniques have led to considerable improvement of grain quality, disease resistance, and productivity of agricultural crops. Who is he?
   (a) E.V. Krishnamurthy
   (b) K.R. Parthasarathy
   (c) C.N.R. Rao (d) B.R. Murthy

439. Though not so famous in India as in the West, this simple Indian mathematician always played with numbers. Who was he?
   (a) S.S. Joshi (b) M.N. Khatri
   (c) D.R. Kaprekar (d) B.S. Rao

440. Which freedom fighter was originally a mathematician?
   (a) Vallabhbhai Patel (b) Lala Hardayal
   (c) Subhas Chandra Bose
   (d) V.D. Savarkar

441. Which mathematician's birth centenary was celebrated in India in 1987?
    (a) P.C. Mahalanobis   (b) S. Ramanujan
    (c) Ram Chandra   (d) Bhaskara

442. Who is the first Indian mathematician to make contributions to the theory of relativity?
    (a) P.C. Vaidya   (b) V.V. Narlikar
    (c) B.C. Mukherjee   (d) Narasinga Rao

443. Initially, the eminent mathematician P.C. Mahalanobis impressed the Government by virtue of his statistical prediction of this aspect of India. Which one?
    (a) Population   (b) Floods
    (c) Food production   (d) Diseases

444. He is the pioneer in applying mathematical and statistical tools to estimate geological sediments and ore deposits. Who is he?
    (a) J.G. Negi   (b) K.S. Valdiya
    (c) K. Chandrasekharan
    (d) B.K. Sahu

445. He has made significant mathematical contributions to the understanding of plasma, the fourth state of matter. Who is he?
    (a) Inder Bir Singh Passi (b) U.R. Rao
    (c) K.G. Ramanathan   (d) S.K. Trehan

446. A recipient of Padma Bhushan, he applied mathematics to the understanding of stars and plasma. Who is he?
    (a) B.N. Prasad (b) S.S. Shirkhande
    (c) P.L. Bhatnagar (d) C.S. Seshadri

447. Who is the pioneer in the education, research, and application of computer science in the country?
    (a) S. Raghavan (b) V. Rajaraman
    (c) E.V. Krishnamurthy
    (d) Rajendra Pawar

448. Which Indian state's cultural tradition of figure-drawing on the threshold of their houses by women contains interesting mathematical ideas now being explored by computer scientists?
    (a) Maharashtra (b) West Bengal
    (c) Tamil Nadu (d) All

449. His most celebrated contribution has been to disprove one of the well-known conjectures of the great mathematician Leonhard Euler. Who is he?
    (a) V.S. Hazurbazar
    (b) S.S. Shrikhande
    (c) G.S. Mahajani
    (d) M.K. Singal

450. Which mathematical text did Srinivasa Ramanujan read during his early years ?
    (a) *Element of Applied Mathematics*
    (b) *Lectures on Elementary Mathematics*
    (c) *Trigonometry and Double Algebra*
    (d) *A Synopsis of Elementary Results in Pure and Applied Mathematics*

451. Who said, 'As the sun eclipses the stars by its brilliancy, so the man of knowledge will eclipse the fame of others in assemblies of the people if he proposes algebraic problems, and still more if he solves them'?
    (a) Bhaskara   (b) Varahamihira
    (c) Aryabhata   (d) Brahmagupta

452. Which great leader of pre-Independent India began his career as a researcher in mathematics?
    (a) Ashutosh Mukherjee
    (b) G.K. Gokhale
    (c) Raja Ram Mohun Roy
    (d) B.G. Tilak

453. Who is the author of the classic *History of Hindu Mathematics*?
    (a) Ram Behari
    (b) B.Dutta and A.N. Singh
    (c) A.K.Bag   (d) Joseph Needham

Mathematics

454. What is 'algebra' in ancient Indian mathematics?
   - (a) *Pati-ganita*
   - (b) *Bija-ganita*
   - (c) *Chakra-ganita*
   - (d) *Tantra-ganita*

455. What was 1/15 called in ancient Indian mathematics?
   - (a) *Panchama*
   - (b) *Panchadasha-bhaga*
   - (c) *Tribhanga*
   - (d) *Tryamsa*

456. In which ancient Indian work were word numerals with place value mentioned for the first time?
   - (a) *Trisatika*
   - (b) *Brihat-Samhita*
   - (c) *Agni-Purana*
   - (d) *Surya-Siddhanta*

457. How much was a 'samudra' equivalent to?
   - (a) 10^2
   - (b) 10
   - (c) 10^9
   - (d) 10^8

458. Zero is denoted by several names in ancient India. Which one is the odd one?
   - (a) *Gagana*
   - (b) *Sunya*
   - (c) *Gati*
   - (d) *Kha*

459. How much was a 'sahasra' equivalent to?
   - (a) 10^6
   - (b) 10^3
   - (c) 10^{11}
   - (d) 10^{12}

460. Which type of numerals has an Indian origin?
- (a) Kharosthi numerals
- (b) Hieratic numerals
- (c) Demotic numerals
- (d) Brahmi numerals

461. How much was an 'ayuta' equivalent to?
- (a) 10^2
- (b) 10^4
- (c) 10^{11}
- (d) 10^{10}

462. What is the ancient Indian name of mathematics?
- (a) *Ganita*
- (b) *Samkhyana*
- (c) *Apara-vidya*
- (d) *Ganana*

463. What is the equivalent of one 'koti'?
- (a) 10^{12}
- (b) 10^8
- (c) 10^7
- (d) 10^3

464. Which ancient Indian's text contains the famous 'Pascal's triangle'?
- (a) Pingala
- (b) Mahavira
- (c) Baudhayana
- (d) Sridara

XIV

MISCELLANY

Humour

465. Who said caustically, 'The different branches of arithmetic – Ambition, Distraction, Uglification, and Derision'?
    - (a) Isaac Newton
    - (b) Lewis Caroll
    - (c) Euclid
    - (d) A.N. Whitehead

466. Who showed to the French philosopher Denis Diderot that God exists by mumbling some mathematical formulae?
    - (a) Francis Bacon
    - (b) Leonhard Euler
    - (c) Georg F. Riemann
    - (d) Augustin Jean Fresnel

467. Who said, 'The mathematician is like a Frenchman: you tell him something, he translates it into his own language, and at once it becomes something altogether different'?
   (a) Aristotle
   (b) Johann von Goethe
   (c) P.B. Shelley
   (d) Richard Dedekind

468. A Greek school of thought laughed at some of Euclid's theorems claiming that even an ass knows them because of their obvious contents. Which school of thought was it?
   (a) Epicurean   (b) Pythagorean
   (c) Aristotelian   (d) Platonic

469. Who said, 'It is one thing to execute a construction by tongue as it were, quite another to carry it out with instruments in hand'?
   (a) Euclid   (b) John Venn
   (c) Jacob Steiner   (d) Albert Girard

470. Which famous mathematician's name literally means 'Son of a Simpleton'?
   (a) Leonardo da Fibonacci
   (b) Diophantus
   (c) Diocles   (d) Pappus

471. Who remarked, 'I never used a logarithm in my life, and could not undertake to extract the square root of four without misgivings'?
    (a) Jawaharlal Nehru   (b) G.B. Shaw
    (c) Alfred Nobel   (d) Winston Churchill

472. What is jokingly referred to as the 'Gangster law of growth'?
    (a) Geometric progression
    (b) Exponential law
    (c) Arithmetic progression
    (d) None

473. Who made this pun on probability : 'He who has heard the same thing told by 12,000 eye-witnesses has only 12,000 probabilities, which are equal to one strong probability, which is far from certainty'?
    (a) George Orwell
    (b) Oliver Wendel Holmes
    (c) Voltaire
    (d) Mary Shelley

474. Who called infinitesimals as 'ghosts of departed quantities'?
    (a) Bishop Berkeley   (b) Johannes Kepler
    (c) St. Thomas Aquinas
    (d) Gaspard Monge

475. Who said, 'God exists since mathematics is consistent, and the Devil exists since we cannot prove it'?
   (a) G.B. Shaw   (b) David Thoreau
   (c) S. Ramanujan   (d) Andre Weil

476. Who used to always remark, 'I was x years old in the year x^2', whenever anybody asked either his age or his year of birth?
   (a) Augustus De Morgan
   (b) George Boole
   (c) Pierre Simon Laplace
   (d) Alexender Macfarlane

477. Who remarked, 'Mathematics is all well and good, but Nature keeps dragging us around by the nose'?
   (a) Roger Penrose
   (b) Stephen Hawking
   (c) Richard Dedekind
   (d) Albert Einstein

478. 'Here is man who would study the stars and cannot see what lies at his feet,' said an old lady when she saw a mathematician and astronomer falling into a well. Who was that mathematician?
   (a) Thales   (b) Anaximander
   (c) Anaxagoras   (d) Imhotep

479. Who said, 'There are three kinds of lies : lies, damned lies, and statistics'?
   (a) Benjamin Disraeli
   (b) Winston Churchill
   (c) Upton Sinclair
   (d) Benjamin Franklin

480. Who disdained infinitesimals and described them as 'a cholera bacillus that threatens to infect all mathematics'?
   (a) Abraham Robinson   (b) G.W. Leibniz
   (c) Georg Cantor   (d) Louis Pasteur

481. Who said, 'It is easier to square the circle than to get round a mathematician'?
   (a) Augustus de Morgan
   (b) Aaron Levenstein
   (c) Thales
   (d) Aristotle

Institutes, Societies and Awards

482. Where is India's premier research centre in mathematics, Institute of Mathematical Sciences, located?
   (a) Mumbai   (b) Chennai
   (c) Pune   (d) New Delhi

483. Which scientific body publishes the reputed *Indian Journal of Pure and Applied Mathematics*?
(a) Indian Association for the Cultivation of Science
(b) Indian Academy of Science
(c) Indian National Science Academy
(d) Indian Institute of Science

484. Which is the first society founded exclusively for the cause of mathematics?
(a) Edinburgh Mathematical Society
(b) London Mathematical Society
(c) The Analytical Society
(d) Societe Mathematique de France

485. Which Indian scientific body awards the S. Ramanujan Medal for original contributions to mathematics and other physical sciences?
(a) I.N.S.A.   (b) I.S.C.A.
(c) D.S.T.   (d) D.S.I.R.

486. Who was the first Indian mathematician to be elected a Fellow of the Royal Society, London?
(a) P.C. Mahalanobis   (b) C.R. Rao
(c) R.C. Bose   (d) S. Ramanujan

487. Where is the Institute of Agricultural Research Statistics located in India?
(a) Kolkata   (b) New Delhi
(c) Hyderabad   (d) Bhopal

488. Which Indian scientific body awards the S.S. Bhatnagar Prize every year for contributions to mathematics?
   (a) C.S.I.R.   (b) D.S.I.R.
   (c) D.S.T.   (d) No such prize exist

489. Which institute or society was the first to start publishing a journal exclusively devoted to mathematics?
   (a) American Mathematical Society
   (b) Ecole Polytechnique
   (c) London Mathematical Society
   (d) Bordeaux Scientific Society

490. Who founded the Indian Statistical Institute, Kolkata, the premier body of its kind in India?
   (a) C.R. Rao   (b) V.S. Hazurbazar
   (c) P.C. Mahalanobis   (d) S.S. Shrikhande

491. Who is the first Indian statistician to be elected a Fellow of the Royal Society, London?
   (a) C.R. Rao   (b) R.C. Bose
   (c) K.B. Madhava   (d) P.C. Mahalanobis

492. Where is the Harish Chandra Institute of Mathematics located?
   (a) Lucknow   (b) Meerut
   (c) Nagpur   (d) Allahabad

493. Which is the highest award of the International Mathematical Union bestowed on a person for his outstanding contribution to mathematics?
    (a) Copley medal   (b) Field's medal
    (c) Fisher's medal   (d) Russell's medal

494. Where was the Ramanujan Institute of Mathematics located once?
    (a) Tiruchirapalli   (b) Trivandrum
    (c) Lucknow   (d) Chennai

495. The Mahalanobis Memorial Medal, named after the great Indian mathematician, is awarded to a person for his contribution to this subject. Which one?
    (a) Statistics   (b) Econometrics
    (c) Sociometrics   (d) Biometry

496. Where is the National Centre for Software Technology – India's premier software institute – located?
    (a) Bangalore   (b) Mumbai
    (c) Hyderabad   (d) Chandigarh

497. Where is the Centre for Development of Advanced Computing located?
    (a) Pune   (b) New Delhi
    (c) Hyderabad   (d) Bangalore

Other than Mathematics

498. He considered himself an 'irreconcilable enemy of kings', embraced revolution and organised several military campaigns. Who was this mathematician?
   - (a) Gaspard Monge
   - (b) Lazare Carnot
   - (c) Charles Dupin
   - (d) Jean Victor Poncelet

499. Where did the Pregel river figure in mathematics?
   - (a) Reauleaux Triangle
   - (b) Seven Bridges of Konigsberg
   - (c) Triangulation of Hanover
   - (d) Stones of Broughm Bridge

500. Which deadly disease is believed to have caused the early death of S. Ramanujan?
   - (a) Malaria
   - (b) Tuberculosis
   - (c) Small-pox
   - (d) Diphtheria

501. Which mathematician died at a young age fighting a dual?
   - (a) Evariste Galois
   - (b) George Polya
   - (c) Leonhard Euler
   - (d) None

502. Which mathematician said that mathematics is a young man's game?
   - (a) Albert Elinstein
   - (b) G.H. Hardy
   - (c) Norbert Wiener
   - (d) Hermann von Helmholtz

503. Which mathematician died at the young age of 26 due to illness?
   (a) Evariste Galois   (b) Niels Henrik Abel
   (c) J.J. Sylvester   (d) Henri Poincare

504. Which mathematician committed suicide for fear of charges of homosexuality?
   (a) Felix Klein   (b) Alan Turing
   (c) David Hilbert   (d) G.H. Hardy

505. Which woman mathematician wrote all her mathematical papers under a male pen name?
   (a) Sofya Kovalevskaya (b) Sophie Germain
   (c) Emmy Neother   (d) All

General

506. Which is the newly emerging field in mathematics and information science?
   (a) Fractals   (b) Bioinformatics
   (c) Chaos   (d) All

507. Which field of science is producing such a huge amount of data that it needs computers to process and analyse it?
   (a) Molecular biology   (b) Genetic engineering
   (c) Evolutionary biology (d) All

508. What is the purpose of the 'Eratosthenes' sieve'?
    (a) Drawing geometrical figures.
    (b) Obtaining prime numbers.
    (c) Eliminating odd numbers.
    (d) Searching for even numbers.

509. What does this mnemonic – an aid to remember
    something – represent: Now, I want a drink
    alcoholic of course after the silly mnemonic?
    (a) Value of π (pi)
    (b) Value of e
    (c) Value of Cos 60 degree
    (d) Value of Sin 30 degree

510. Which subject nowadays finds wide applications in
    various sciences, namely, physics, meteorology,
    biology, medicine and finance?
    (a) Mathematical modelling
    (b) Statistics
    (c) Calculus
    (d) Non-Euclidean geometry

511. From the mathematical point of view, what is
    mankind drawing close to?
    (a) Computer Era   (b) Robotics Era
    (c) Information Era   (d) Non-Euclidean Era

512. What is applied mathematics?
    (a) Mathematics in the real world.
    (b) The real, rather than abstract mathematics.
    (c) Application of mathematics of real world problems.
    (d) All.

513. What is 'higher mathematics'?
    (a) Mathematics of specialised kind.
    (b) Mathematics of greater abstraction.
    (c) Mathematics taught at college level.
    (d) Mathematics at the frontier of knowledge.

514. What is known as 'new maths'?
    (a) The principles of set theory introduced at an elementary level.
    (b) A new method of teaching mathematics.
    (c) Mathematics taught as fun and play.
    (d) None.

515. What is known as 'pure mathematics'?
    (a) The study of mathematical systems and structure in the abstract.
    (b) The study of mathematics systems and structure for their applications.
    (c) The study of abstraction in mathematics.
    (d) All.

516. What is 'Ulam's dilemma'?
   (a) A mathematician cannot keep track of some not to speak of all the activity taking place in mathematics.
   (b) Whether the world is real or a mathematical entity.
   (c) Whether or not mathematics alone can explain the world.
   (d) Whether or not a mathematician alone can explain the world.

517. What is 'Buffon's needle'?
   (a) A statistical experiment.
   (b) A mathematical game.
   (c) A puzzle involving geometry.
   (d) An unsolved problem.

518. The life of the Princeton mathematician and Nobel Laureate John Nash has been made into an Oscar-winning major film. Which is it?
   (a) *A Beautiful Mind*
   (b) *Ek Doctor Ki Mauth*
   (c) *The Ambassador*   (d) *None*

519. Which is the novel computer invented in India to cater to the needs of an average Indian?
   (a) Param   (b) Simputer
   (c) Avishkar   (d) Agni

520. What is the term used to describe advances made in computers?
    (a) Step   (b) Generation
    (c) Mark   (d) Jump

XV

PHOTO QUIZ

The computers shown in the following photos are important milestones in the history of computer. Can you identify these milestones?

521.

522.

523.

524.

525.

ANSWERS

1.(a) and (c)

2.(c) The ABC (Atanasoff-Berry Computer)

3.(d)   4.(b)   5.(c)

6.(a) Often, Pascal is given this credit.

7.(b)

8.(c) Argand however put the idea on a firm footing.

9.(b)   10.(c)   11.(b)

12.(a)

13.(d) Claimed the value lay between 223/71 and 22/7.

14.(b)   15.(a)   16.(d)

17.(b)   18.(d)   19.(b)

20.(a)   21.(a)   22.(c)

23.(a) To be precise, Alternating Current.

24.(a) An abundant number is less than the sum of its factors excluding itself.

25.(c)

26.(a) Francois Viete is the author.

27.(a) Composite number has factors.

28.(b)   29.(a)   30.(d)

31.(d)   32.(a)   33.(a)

34.(a)   35.(d)   36.(d)

37.(b)Broughm Bridge on the Royal Canal in Dublin, Ireland.

38.(b)   39.(b)   40.(a)

41.(c)   42.(b)   43.(d)

44.(b)   45.(c)   46.(c)

47.(d)

48.(a) Wrote massive tomes on mathematics in a clear, methodical style.

49.(d)   50.(b)   51.(b)

52.(d)   53.(c)   54.(c)

55.(d)   56.(c)   57.(b)

58.(d)

59.(b) Called 'Polyhedron' generally.

60.(d)	61.(a)	62.(c)
63.(b)	64.(b)	65.(a)
66.(c)		

67.(b) Sometimes called 'Menger sponge'.

68.(a)	69.(b)	

70.(a) Called 'Sylvester's Bicorn'.

71.(a)	72.(a)	73.(a)
74.(a)	75.(c) Called 'Euler's Deltoid'.	
76.(c)	77.(c)	78.(a)
79.(b)	80.(d)	81.(b)
82.(b)		

83.(b) Water waves, electromagnetic waves, sound waves, etc, follow this.

84.(a)

85.(b) Often called 'Rose of Grandi'.

86.(d) A subject of bitter quarrel amongst mathematicians.

87.(c)

88.(d) Formed by joining the feet of the perpendiculars from any given point to the sides.

89.(b) and (d)	90.(a)	91.(d)
92.(a)	93.(d)	94.(a)

95.(a) Triangle made of three intersecting arcs of circles.

96.(c)	97.(c)

98.(d) These triples are of the type $x^2 + y^2 = z^2$, where x, y and z are Pythagorean triples.

99.(c)	100.(c)	101.(d)
102.(b)	103.(a)	

104.(b) When an n digit Kaprekar number is squared and the right-hand n-digits are added to the left-hand n or n-1 digits the result is the original number.

105.(a) Hindu numerals reached Europe via the Arab.

106.(d)

107.(d) These numbers are sums of the preceding three numbers.

108.(b)   109.(d)   110.(b)

111.(b)   112.(a)   113.(b)

114.(b)

115.(a) 'Arithmetike' means a number science.

116.(a)

117.(a) Also used for checking additions or subtractions.

118.(a)   119.(a)   120.(c)

121.(c) Mohammed ibn Musa al-Khowarizmi. Al-Khowarizmi became algorithm.

122.(d)   123.(d)   124.(b)   This terminology exists in the USA and France. In the UK it is equal to 10^{42}.

125.(a)

126.(d) This terminology exists in the USA and France. In the UK it is equal to 10^{18}.

127.(c) This terminology exists in the USA and France. In the UK, it is equal to 10^{36}.

128.(a)   129.(d)

130.(a) This terminology is prevalent in the USA and France. In the UK and Germany, it is equal to 10^{12}.

131.(d) This terminology is prevalent in the USA and France. In the UK, it is equal to 10^{24}.

132.(c) This terminology is prevalent in the USA and France. In the UK, it is equal to 10^{30}.

133.(a)   134.(c)   135.(a)

136.(c) This terminology is prevalent in the USA and France. In the UK, it is equal to 10^{48}.

137.(c)   138.(c)   139.(a)

140.(b)   141.(c)   142.(b)

143.(d)   144.(a) One million.

145.(c)   146.(b)   147.(c)

148.(d)   149.(c)   150.(d)

151.(b)   152.(a) and (d)

153.(a) Still unproved.

154.(c)	155.(a)	156.(b)
157.(a)	158.(a)	159.(d)
160.(b)	161.(c)	162.(b)
163.(b)	164.(d)	165.(c)
166.(b)	167.(a)	168.(a)
169.(d)	170.(b)	171.(b)

172.(b) $4,913 = 17^3$.   173.(b) Each Fibonacci number is the sum of the two previous numbers.

174.(d) All approximate because e irrational.

175.(a) Each number is the sum of the proper divisors of the other.

176.(b) A perfect number is the sum of its divisors, including unity but excluding itself.

177.(a)

178.(d) All approximate because π (pi) is an irrational number.

179.(d) A product of seven 2s.

180.(a) They form an amicable pair.

181.(b)	182.(b)	183.(b)

184.(d)

185.(a) $132 = 13+32+21+31+23+12$

186.(b)

187.(a) $3^2 + 3^2 + 3^2 = 5^2 + 1^2 + 1^2 = 27$.

188.(d) $50 = 5^2 + 5^2 = 7^2 + 1^2$.

189.(c) $31 = 1 + 2 + 2^2 + 2^3 + 2^4 = 1 + 5 + 5^2$.

190.(c) $145 = 11 + 41 + 51$.

191.(c) $216 = 3^3 + 4^3 + 5^3$.

192.(b) $251 = 1^3 + 5^3 + 5^3 = 2^3 + 3^3 + 6^3$.

193.c) $1^2 + 18^2$, $6^2 + 17^2$ and $10^2 + 15^2$

194.(d)	195.(a)	196.(b)
197.(a)	198.(b)	

199.(d) $2E4 = (2 \times 12\,2) + (11 \times 12) + (4 \times 12\,0) = 424$

200.(b)	201.(b)	202.(d)
203.(d)	204.(c)	205.(b)

206.(b)   207.(c)   208.(a)
209.(d)   210.(a)   211.(a)
212.(b)
213.(a)The sum of rows, columns and diagonals of the smallest magic square.
214.(d) Composed of numbers 1 to 19.
215.(c) Composed of 144 odd primes from 3 onwards.
216.(a)   217.(b)   218.(b)
219.(a)   220.(c)   221.(d)
222.(d)   223.(d)   224.(a)
225.(b)   226.(c)   227.(b)
228.(d)   229.(d)   230.(a)
231.(b)   232.(b)   233.(c)
234.(b)   235.(b)   236.(a)
237.(c) Knots are symmetrical 'mirror images' of one another and so are topologically equivalent.
238.(c)
239.(a) Called 'Penrose tassellation' after its inventor, Roger Penrose.
240.(b) After David Hilbert who conceived them.
241.(b) Known after its creator, H. von Koch, it is closely associated with measurement of a coastline.
242.(b)   243.(b)   244.(a)
245.(d) This fundamental set is associated with fractual geometry.
246.(b)   247.(b)
248.(c)   249.(d)   250.(b)
251.(a)   252.(b)
253.(a) Problem was posed by a gambler to Blaise Pascal. But it was solved independently both by Pascal and Pierre de Fermat.
254.(c)   255.(c)   256.(d)
257.(d)   258. John Napier
259. Rene Descartes
260. Niels Henrik Abel
261. Norbert Wiener   262. George Stibitz

263. Carl F. Gauss   264. George Boole
265. D.R.Kaprekar
266. Alan Turing
267. Bertrand Russell
268. Felix Klein
269. Sofya Kovalevsky
270. G.W.Leibniz   271.Howard H. Aiken
272. Raj Reddy   273.(b)   274.(c)
275. (c)   276.(a)   277.(b)
278. (d)   279.(b)   280.(c)
281. (d)   282.(a)   283.(b)
284. (c)   285.(c)   286.(a)
287.(a)

288.(b) Installed in England during the Second World War.
289.(c) Called 'Wheel and disc integrator', it was used in Vannevar
Bush's Differential Analyser.
290.(d)   291.(a)   292.(d)
293.(a)   294.(c)
295.(c) Eratosthenes made this estimate which was 38,400 km.

296.(b) William Harvey did that calculation.
297.(a) and (c)
298.(b) An asteroid discovered by Joseph Piazzi but soon mislaid
until its precise position predicted by Carl F. Gauss.   299.(d)
300. (a) Titius-Bode law discovered by Johann E. Bode in 1772.
301.(a)   302.(a) and (d)   303.(a)   304.(d)
305.(b)
306. (a) Led to discovery of fusion energy and hydrogen bomb.
307. (d)   308.(d)
309. (b) The phrase referred to the problem of accommodating a
large number of electric and electronic components within a given
space for an electronic equipment or gadget.
310.(a)   311.(c)   312.(a)
313.(c)   314.(b)   315.(b)

316. (a)   317.(a) and (c)
318.(d) More popular as 'Lissajous figures'.
319.(a)   320.(b)   321.(c)
322.(a)   323.(a)   324.(c)
325.(d)   326.(b)   327.(c)
328.(b)   329.(a)   330.(b)
331.(a)   332.(a)   333.(a)
334.(b)   335.(c)
336.(a) Its author is Russell Maloney.
337.(d)   338.(d)
339.(b) Those mysterious numbers are called 'Plato numbers' after its author, Plato.
340.(c)   341.(c)   342.(a)
343.(b) The author is Lewis Padgett.
344.(a) Called 'Tristram Shandy paradox', a paradox of the infinite.
345.(c) The author is Robert M. Coates.
346.(a) The author is Joseph Lagrange.
347.(c)   348.(c)   349.(b)
350.(b) Its engraver was Albrecht Durer.
351.(c)   352.(b)   353.(b)
354.(b) His contemporary Duccio was also a pioneer of the same technique of art.
355.(c)   356.(d)   357.(c)
358.(b)   359.(d)   360.(d)
361.(b) Platonism, Formalism and Constructivism.
362.(a)   363.(d)   364.(b)
365.(c) At one time it was thought that it is as obvious that God exists as the sum of angles in a triangle is 180 degree. In non-Euclidean geometry, the sum of angles in a triangle could be equal to, less than or greater than, 180 degree. All ethical and moral values are therefore subject to situations and circumstances.
366.(c) According to this school, mathematics is a play of symbols, which exhibits a structure that has useful applications.
367.(c)

368.(a) According to this school, mathematics is a branch of logic.

369.(c)	370.(b)	371.(c)
372.(b)	373.(c)	374.(a)
375.(c)	376.(d)	377.(b)
378.(c)	379.(a)	

380.(c) These written records are of about 250 B.C. However, they do not contain zero and do not use position value notation.

381.(a)	382.(d)	383.(d)
384.(b)	385.(b)	386.(a)
387.(c)	388.(a)	389.(b)
390.(a)	391.(d)	392.(a)
393.(b)	394.(c)	

395.(c) Unearthed by a farmer in 1818, the contents of the manuscript are believed to be no later than of the fourth century.

396.(b)	397.(a)	398.(b)
399.(d) A Chinese text.		400.(b)
401.(c)		

402.(b) To be precise, Pythagoreans had this motto.

403.(a)	404.(a)

405.(b) Known after G.A.Plimpton collection at Columbia University. It contains Pythagorean triples.

406.(b)	407.(c)	408.(b)
409.(c)	410.(a)	411.(d)
412.(c)		

413.(d) The earliest known magic square in the world – Lo Shu. Constructed about 1000 B.C.in China.

414.(d)	415.(b)

416.(d) Proved to date only for integers less than 30,000.

417.(a)	418.(b)	419.(a)
420.(d)	421.(a)	422.(a)
423.(c)	424.(b)	425.(b)
426.(b)	427.(d)	

428.(a) Wirtten in about 300 B.C., its author was Kautilya.

429.(b) Ram Chandra's books on mathematics were published in England in about 1860.

430.(b)	431.(b)	432.(d)
433.(b)	434.(c)	435.(b)
436.(a)	437.(c)	438.(d)
439.(c)	440.(b)	441.(b)
442.(b)	443.(b)	444.(d)
445.(d)	446.(c)	447.(b)

448.(c) Called 'Kolam'.

449.(b) In collaboration with R.C.Bose and Parker, Shrikhande made this celebrated discovery. This trio was nicknamed 'Euler's spoilers'.

450.(d) Its author is G.S.Carr.

451.(d)

452.(a) Tilak was also a mathematician.

453.(b)	454.(b)	455.(b)
456.(c)	457.(c)	458.(c)
459.(b)	460.(d)	461.(b)
462.(a)	463.(c)	

464.(a) 'Chandah-Sutra' written about 200 B.C. much earlier than any European source.

465.(b) Original name Charles Lutwidge Dodgson, a mathematician.

466.(b)	467.(b)	468.(a)
469.(c)		

470.(a) His father was nicknamed 'Bonaccio' meaning 'Simpleton'.

471.(b)	472.(a) and (b)	
473.(c)	474.(a)	475.(d)
476.(a)	477.(d)	478.(a)
479.(a)	480.(c)	481.(a)
482.(b)	483.(c)	
484.(b) Founded in 1865.		485.(a)
486.(d)	487.(b)	488.(a)
489.(b)	490.(c)	491.(d)

492.(d)

493.(b) Named after a Canadian analyst.

494.(d)	495.(b)	496.(b)
497.(a)	498.(b)	499.(b)
500.(b)	501.(a)	502.(b)
503.(b)	504.(b)	505.(b)
506.(b)	507.(d)	508.(b)

509.(a) π (pi) = 3.141 592 653 58 (each word corresponds to digit).

510.(a)	511.(c)

512.(c)

513.(b) For example, topology, number theory, analysis, etc.

514.(a)	515.(a)

516.(a) Named after Stanislaw Ulam who described his dilemma.

517.(a) Experiment for determining the value of π (pi) using statistical means.   518.(a)

519.(b) SIMple comPUTER.

520.(b)

521. Zuse-IV built by Konrad Zuse in Germany in about 1943.

522. The Differential Analyser invented by Vannevar Bush at Massachussetts Institute of Technology, USA.

523.Supercomputer Cray X-M.P. invented by Seymour Cray built about 1972 in the USA.

524.Model of Charles Babbage's 'Difference Engine'. Started construction in England in 1823 but was not completed.

525.The Indian-made supercomputer 'PARAM-10000' built by Centre for Development of Advanced Computing, Pune.

SCORE YOURSELF!

Count the correct answers you have given and mark yourself as follows:

Average: if 450-474 answers are correct.

Good: if 475-499 answers are correct.

Excellent: if 500-524 answers are correct.

If you score more than 525, you are a SUPER EXPERT in Maths.